SKELETON KEYS

THE
HAUNTING
OF LUNA MOON

To my family ~ Guy Bass

To Mum, Dad & Lynne – thank you!

~ Pete Williamson

STRIPES PUBLISHING LIMITED

An imprint of the Little Tiger Group
1 Coda Studios, 189 Munster Road,
London SW6 6AW

A paperback original
First published in Great Britain in 2020

ISBN: 978-1-78895-104-3

A CIP catalogue record for this book is available
from the British Library.

Printed and bound in the UK.

The Forest Stewardship Council® (FSC®) is a global, not-for-profit organization
dedicated to the promotion of responsible forest management worldwide.
FSC® defines standards based on agreed principles for responsible forest stewardship that
are supported by environmental, social, and economic stakeholders.
To learn more, visit www.fsc.org

2 4 6 8 10 9 7 5 3 1

SKELETON KEYS

THE HAUNTING OF LUNA MOON

WRITTEN BY
GUY BASS

ILLUSTRATED BY
PETE WILLIAMSON

stripes

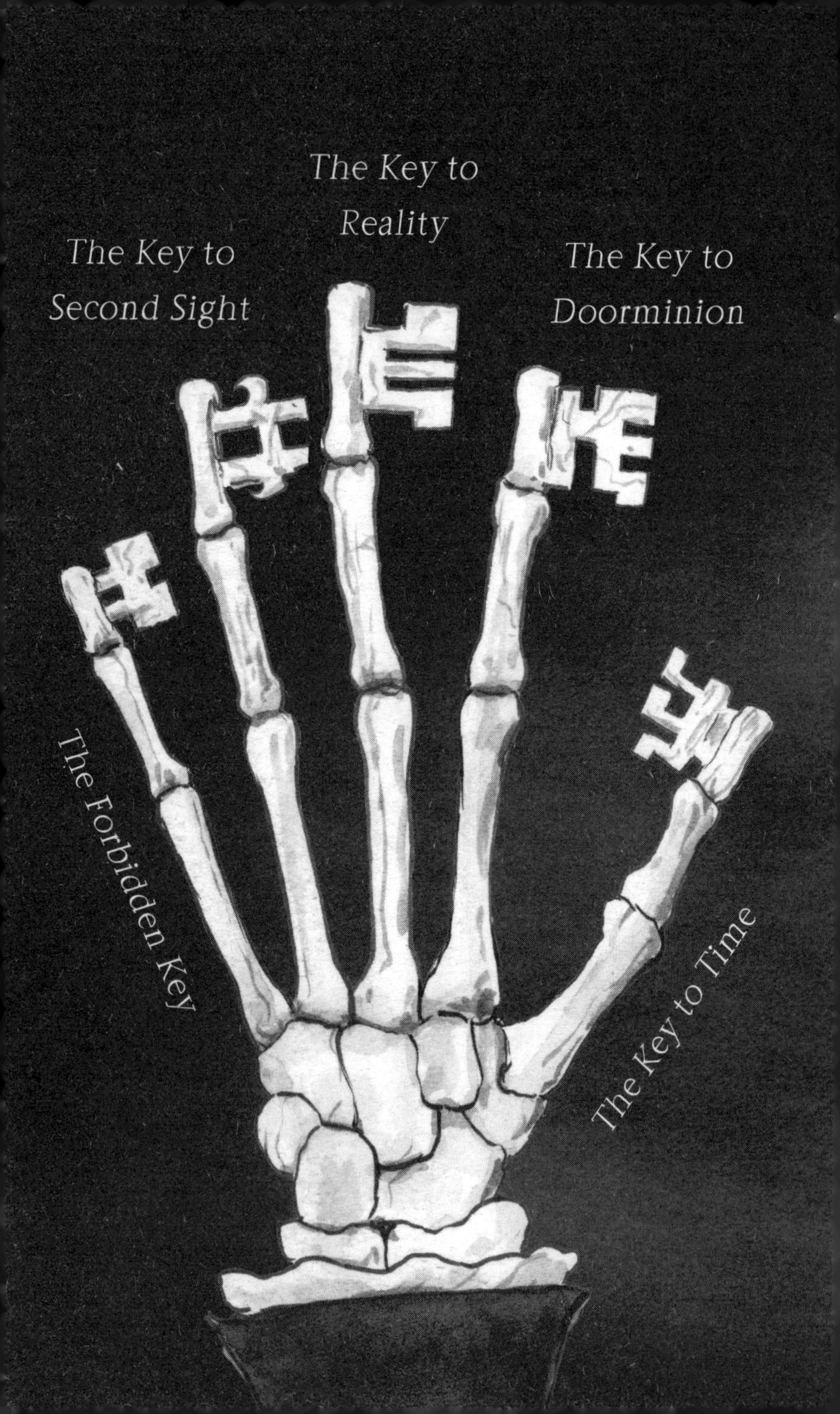

The Key to
Reality

The Key to
Second Sight

The Key to
Doorminion

The Forbidden Key

The Key to Time

The Key to
Possibility

The Key to
a Quick Getaway

The Key to
the Kingdom

The Key to Imagination

The Key to Oblivion

reetings! To waffleboggers, figswindlers and joustabouts! To the imaginary and the unimaginary! To the living, the dead and everyone in between, my name is Keys ... Skeleton Keys.

A long time ago and not at all recently, I was an IF – an imaginary friend. But by some wonder of wild imagining I suddenly became as real as sticks! I had become *unimaginary*.

Today I keep a watchful eye socket on the recently unimagined, wherever they appear. For with these fantabulant fingers I can open doors to anywhere and beyond ... hidden worlds ... secret places ... doors to the limitless realm of all the imagination.

Mark my words, Ol' Mr Keys has opened more doors than you have had biscuits – and each door has led to an adventure that would make a head spin from its neck! The stories I could tell you...

But of course *stories* are why you are here! Well, sit back and relax – because I have a hum-dum-dinger of a tale set to send your thoughts running for cover. A story so truly unbelievable that it must, unbelievably, be true.

Our tale begins many moons ago in Haggard Hall – a great, looming shadow of a house far from anywhere. In Haggard Hall there lived a boy. This boy was alone, with no one to care for him and only his wild imagination for company. Haggard Hall was as lonely as darkness and so, in time, the boy imagined he had a friend. He named his IF Mr Malarkey, for a fantabulant friend, however imaginary, deserves a fantabulant name.

Mr Malarkey was a curious creature – as round as an egg, as splendid as a starry sky and chock-brimming with magic spells and flabbergasting tricks – and he immediately made the boy feel less alone.

Then, one fate-filled, moonish night, the boy imagined his friend so wildly and so well that something rather remarkable happened – Mr Malarkey became as real as noses!

Mr Malarkey's spells and tricks were even more magical and flabbergasting in real life, and all he cared about was making the boy as happy as Christmas.

But the boy was *not happy*. You see, when

Mr Malarkey was all in his head, the boy liked him well enough, but the moment his IF became real, something changed. The boy realized he did not want to share his home with anyone – even a figment of his own imagination. Despite the house being big enough for both of them – big enough for a *hundred* Mr Malarkeys – the boy wanted to be alone again.

And so he sent his unimaginary friend away, banishing him forever from Haggard Hall. But since poor Mr Malarkey had nowhere else to go, he simply vanished in a puff of sadness, never to be seen again.

In time the boy grew into a man, and the man into an old man. Despite his best efforts, the old man did not manage to spend his life alone. He had a family, though he reminded them as often as possible that he would prefer it if they were not there.

I am sure you are cram-bursting at the seams to be introduced to the boy that became known as Old Man Moon. Alas, like a winged cow, it is impossible! For there is one thing about the man I have not told you...

Old Man Moon is quite dead.

Only the old man's granddaughter, Luna, is sorry to see him go. And it is Luna Moon who may be the key to unlocking the mystery of this tall-but-true tale, for strange things can happen when imaginations run wild...

Let us join Luna and the rest of the family at Haggard Hall. It is the dead of winter and Old Man Moon's family has gathered to pay their respects. The funeral may be over, but the old man's story is most certainly not...

CHAPTER ONE

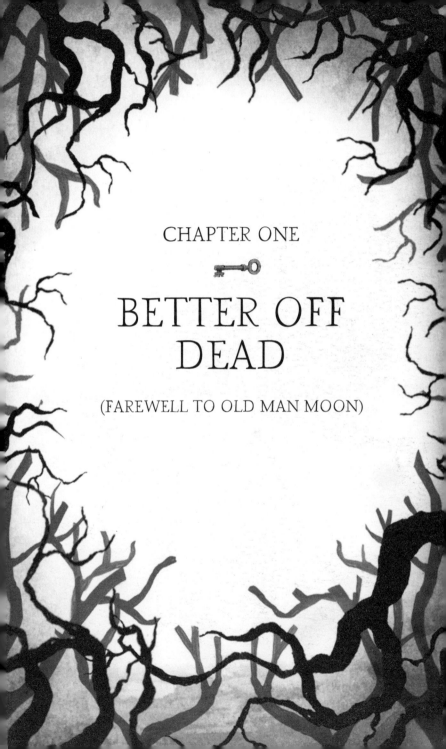

BETTER OFF DEAD

(FAREWELL TO OLD MAN MOON)

Moon Family Tree

Old Man Moon

Ray Moon—Dawn Moon   Summer Moon   Meriwether Moon

Luna Moon   Sonny Moon

"Behind every door, a story waits."
—SK

Night was falling as the Moon family made their way down the snow-covered hill from the chapel to the house. Luna Moon watched her cold breath puff out of her mouth as she followed her family from a distance.

"What an emotional funeral," declared Mum. "I haven't laughed so much in years!"

"I could have danced all night on the old man's grave!" declared Dad.

"Such fun!" chuckled Uncle Meriwether. "The only thing better than saying goodbye..."

"...is saying good riddance!" added Aunt

9

Summer. Luna watched her swing open the hall's great, creaking door and everyone stomped the snow off their boots before they skipped inside the vast, grand hallway, laughing and joking.

"Can we do it again tomorrow?" added Luna's brother, dashing inside.

Like Mum and Dad, Sonny was golden-haired and always looked like he'd just been on holiday. Luna, however, was as pale as paper, with sleepless eyes and a sharp bob of pure white hair. Whiter still was Luna's pet rat, Simon Parker, who perched on her shoulder.

"Granddad's gone, Simon Parker, and everyone's *happy* about it," Luna said to her rat as she lingered in the doorway. "I know he wasn't nice but he was still my granddad."

Luna's rat let out a shivery squeak, keen to return to the relative warmth of Haggard Hall.

"Luna Moon, you're letting all the cold in!" said Mum, rushing back into the snow and taking Luna by the hand. She pulled her inside and slammed the creaking door shut. Mum was tall and willowy, with long hair at least twice as golden as sunshine and a bright white dress that went all the way to the floor.

"Well, we'd better get warmed up then," Aunt Summer noted with a grin, stamping her feet as she paced around the grand hallway. Luna's aunt was short and round and, since she'd also chosen to wear a white dress and coat to Old Man Moon's funeral, reminded Luna of a snowball. Aunt Summer tapped her chin thoughtfully. "And who knows the best way to warm up?"

"Big hugs!" Sonny shouted excitedly.

"Big hugs!" cried everyone except Luna. The family immediately began hugging and squeezing each other as if their lives

depended on it. Simon Parker scuttled off
Luna's shoulder and into the pocket of her
coat just as Mum and Dad swamped Luna
with a double hug. It felt as warm as a goose-
down duvet.

"Luna Mona Moon, have we told you
recently how much we love you?" asked
Mum.

"How much?" Luna asked.

"To the moon and
back," said Dad.
"Always have, always
will."

Luna closed her eyes
as Mum and Dad
held her tightly.
She could have
melted into that
moment and lived
in it forever.

"Well, I for one am *still* not warm enough..."
Aunt Summer declared. She winked at Sonny.
"I wonder what will get the blood flowing...?"

"Jolly Jolly Joy Dance!" squealed Sonny
excitedly.

"Jolly Jolly Joy Dance!" everyone but
Luna shouted.

"No more dancing in secret for this family!"
Aunt Summer exclaimed. "Uncle Meriwether,
some music!"

"Music it is!" chuckled Uncle Meriwether,
who laughed at everything and was always,
always hungry. "And then cake!" he added.
"I'm *starving*..."

As Mum and Dad squeezed the breath
out of her, Luna watched Uncle Meriwether
bounce over to an old record player in the
corner of the hallway. He was even rounder
than Aunt Summer, and between his bushy
white beard and jolliness, Sonny was

convinced he was secretly Father Christmas. Uncle Meriwether chuckled away as he put on a record. A moment later the sound of a jaunty piano band echoed through the house.

"Join in, Luna! There's not been music or dancing in this house for years!" said Aunt Summer. As her aunt took Sonny by the hands and spun him around the room, Luna felt a sudden knot of anger in the pit of her stomach.

"You danced already," she snapped, wriggling out of Mum and Dad's loving embrace. "You danced on Granddad's grave. You all took turns."

"Served him right!" said Aunt Summer.

"The wicked old killjoy!" laughed Uncle Meriwether.

"He was a rotter!" said Dad.

"He was a swine!" said Mum.

"His breath stinked!" shouted Sonny, keen

to join in. By now, the whole family was dancing in a sort of giddy jig as Aunt Summer sang.

"I'm Old Man Moon!
I never let you dance!
I'm Old Man Moon!
I put pepper in your pants!
I'm Old Man Moon!
I made you eat a bee!
I'm Old Man Moon!
I'm dead and you are free!"

Everyone was having a wild-eyed whale of a time – everyone except Luna. Yes, her grandfather was unkind, but Luna was fairly sure he didn't know how to be anything else.

"You shouldn't be happy that someone's gone," muttered Luna as her rat climbed back on to her shoulder. "Not even Granddad."

It was not as if her grandfather had been kind to her. Every week he would try to send her away – to banish her from Haggard Hall.

"Go on, get out! This is my house, not yours … leave me here alone!" the old man would wheeze, even as Luna sat by his bedside. As soon as he had caught his breath he'd add, "I will never leave this house … not even when I die. For I shall haunt these walls … I shall haunt *you* – from beyond the grave. I will haunt you, and it'll serve you right!"

Those words haunted Luna, all right. But she wasn't sure her grandfather really meant what he said. Luna wasn't sure he even really wanted to be alone. Perhaps, she thought, her grandfather was *scared* of being alone. So she stayed by his bedside until her grandfather breathed his last.

But not everyone in her family was as forgiving as Luna.

"Look at me, I'm Old Man Moon! I'm Old Man Moon and I'm better off dead!" laughed Aunt Summer, doing her very best impression of the old man's crooked, back-bent silhouette as she danced up the curved staircase.

For a few moments Luna could hear her
aunt's singing as she disappeared into the
shadows... Then came a sudden cry, and Aunt
Summer was gone.

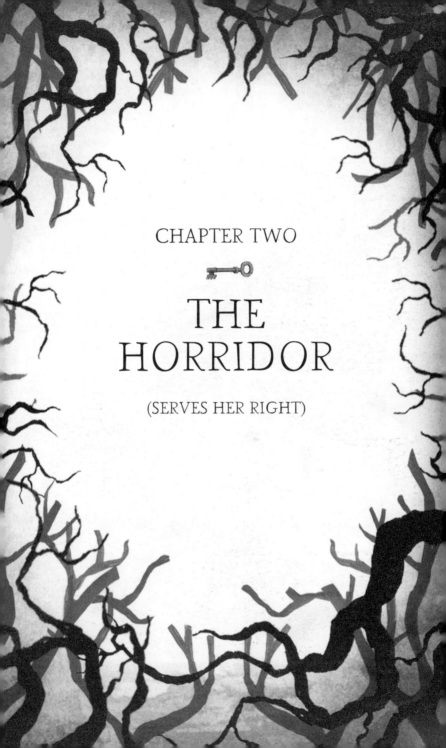

CHAPTER TWO

THE
HORRIDOR

(SERVES HER RIGHT)

"Aunt Summer?" called Luna at the
sound of her aunt's scream. She
looked back at her family, dancing for joy in a
pool of warm light. They hadn't heard a thing
over the echoing music. Luna walked slowly
down the grand hallway, the floor replying
to her footsteps with loud creaks. Before she
reached the staircase at the hallway's far end,
she had to pass by a full-size suit of medieval
armour, which stood in the middle of the
room like an iron sentry. It held a sword in its
metal gauntlet, and a dark plume of feathers

23

protruded from the top of its helmet. The suit of armour had always made Luna oddly nervous, and she found herself hurrying past it to the foot of the stairs. She stared up into darkness and rested her hand on the banister. The wood was smooth and winter-cold.

The rat on her shoulder squeaked nervously.

"What are you worried about, Simon Parker?" Luna said, stroking the rat's head. Being a rat, Simon Parker did not reply, but Luna smiled warmly and he seemed to calm down. Luna always felt better when Simon Parker was around. She first encountered him when she was eight years old – she had been preparing dinner for her grandfather and opened the kitchen cupboard to find the rat crouched between two tins of soup. His fur was as white as Luna's hair and though she had never been a fan of the rats that roamed Haggard Hall, Luna felt a strange affection for this pale creature. Since her grandfather had not allowed pets of any kind in the house, Luna kept Simon Parker a secret, hiding him in the pocket of her coat whenever the old man was around. It was the first secret she had ever kept.

It would not be the last.

"Aunt Summer...?" Luna said in a whisper.

Silence.

Luna crept upstairs. She was swallowed into the gloom as she followed the curve of the banister up to the landing. Moonlight poured in from windows above her, giving everything an ice-blue hue. *Where is she?* Luna thought. A shiver was halfway down her spine, when:

"..."

Luna spun round. She could have sworn she'd heard Aunt Summer's voice, but muffled, as if she was trapped in a cupboard.

"Did you hear that, Simon Parker?" Her rat

scuttled nervously from one shoulder to the other. "Lot of help you are," added Luna and turned slowly towards the sound. Then she saw it:

THE HORRIDOR.

The corridor leading to her grandfather's bedroom stretched out like a bad memory. The door at the far end was barely visible in the darkness. Luna's brother (who was even more scared of Old Man Moon than he was of spiders) had nicknamed it *the horridor* – not just because it was long and somehow even colder than the rest of the house ... not even because the Old Man usually lurked behind the dreaded door, ready to throw an insult or shoe ... but because of the dozens of paintings that covered the walls. Portraits of her grandfather filled the horridor, as if the only company he enjoyed was his own. Since he had refused to smile, the old man looked

the same in every portrait – ancient, sour and scowling ... veins spidering beneath pale, greying skin ... thin lips pressed together in disapproval ... piercing, judgmental eyes.

Did Aunt Summer go into Granddad's room? Luna thought. Since her grandfather, ever the miser, had removed all the bulbs in the horridor, Luna had only the faintest moonlight from the landing to guide her.

She held her breath as she moved slowly towards the door. She heard the CREAK CREEEAK of the floorboards ... felt the burning stares of the portraits. Then:

"..."

Aunt Summer's voice again! Still faint, but ... closer? Simon Parker let out a squeak. Luna was about to reach for the door when the portrait to her left caught her eye. It wasn't like all the others. It didn't have her grandfather's grumpy, grimacing face staring back at her.

In fact, in didn't have her grandfather's face at all.

It was a portrait of Aunt Summer.

How had Luna never noticed it before?
She'd been down this corridor dozens of
times. And why would her grandfather let the
painting hang there? He didn't allow pictures
of anyone other than *himself*. Luna looked
closer. Aunt Summer had an odd, shocked
expression on her face, but odder still was
that she was wearing the same sparkling
white dress and coat that she'd worn to the

funeral. It was as if someone had managed to paint an entire picture of her since Luna had last seen her.

"How...?" Luna mouthed. Then she heard Aunt Summer's voice again, distant and desperate, and looked back at the painting. Her mouth fell open.

The painting had changed. Or rather, Aunt Summer's expression had changed.

She was screaming.

Luna had never seen anyone look so scared. The portrait of Aunt Summer was staring her in the eyes, her mouth open wide.

"*Serves her right,*" hissed a voice.

Luna spun round. There was no one there. The voice had come from nowhere ... but there was no mistaking who it was.

"G-Granddad...?" Luna gasped. She stumbled back down the corridor in surprise ... and felt a hand grab her by the shoulders.

"AAARGH!" she cried. She turned to see Dad's face staring back at her. Behind him stood the rest of the family, wearing equally concerned expressions.

"There you are!" said Dad. "We've been looking for you all over – we can't very well do the Jolly Jolly Joy Dance without our sunbeam!"

"Are you all right, Luna? You look pale. Well, *paler*," said Mum. "What are you doing up here?"

"Hatching a plan with Aunt Summer to steal my cake, no doubt!" chuckled Uncle Meriwether. "Where is your aunt, anyway?"

"He – he got her," Luna whispered. "He got Aunt Summer!"

"What do you mean, 'he got Aunt Summer'?" asked Dad. "Who got her?"

"Granddad," said Luna. "He's come back to haunt us."

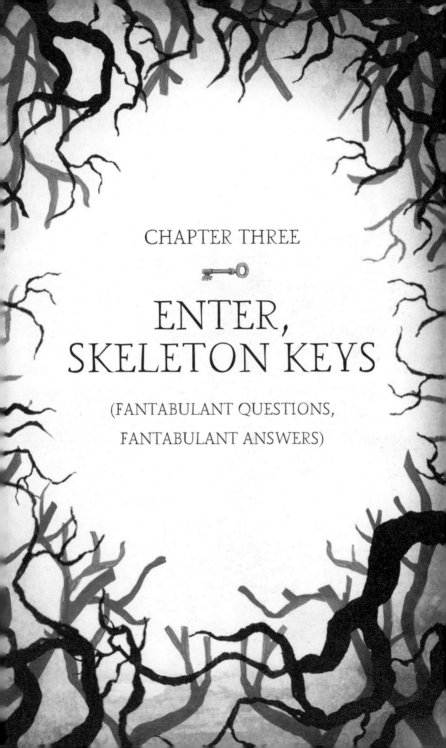

CHAPTER THREE

ENTER, SKELETON KEYS

(FANTABULANT QUESTIONS,
FANTABULANT ANSWERS)

*No wonder Mona Lisa had a mysterious smile
upon her face – who could have suspected she was
Leonardo Da Vinci's unimaginary friend?*

"Granddad came back as a ghost?" Sonny whimpered in panic. "He said he would! He said he'd come back to haunt us and it'd serve us right!"

"Your grandfather has done no such thing," said Mum sternly. "Luna Moon, why would you say that?"

"I heard his voice," Luna said as her rat let out a series of urgent squeaks. "Simon Parker heard it too."

"Now don't be a silly sandwich," said Dad in his serious voice. "Your grandfather is deader than dinosaurs at a disco. There's no coming back from that."

"But—" Luna began.

"Let's not get into but-but-buts," interrupted Mum. She pointed to Old Man Moon's bedroom door. "Your grandfather is no more likely to come back and haunt us than he is to walk through that door."

There was a

CLICK

– then a

CLUNK.

Luna glanced back.

Someone had unlocked the door to the old man's room ... from *inside*.

"G-Granddad...?" Sonny gasped as the door handle slowly turned.

Everyone froze. The only movement was the nervous twitching of Simon Parker's whiskers.

The door creaked open. A figure loomed in the doorway.

"It – it's not possible…" uttered Dad. "It can't be the old man…"

"He's back!" Uncle Meriwether gasped, his voice trembling. "Back from the dead!"

"Dead? Well, I suppose I do look a little *grave*…" said the figure, stepping forwards. He was tall, painfully lean and dressed in a finely tailored suit complete with breeches and a long tailcoat, white stockings and shoes with brightly polished buckles. But where you might reasonably expect to see a human head, the figure had only a creamy-white skull.

It was a skeleton.

Uncle Meriwether was the first to scream. It sounded like a cat being thrown out of a window.

"I get that a lot," the skeleton noted. His

eyeballs, which floated impossibly in the sockets of his skull, stared at each of the family members in turn. "I am afraid skinless is how I came into this world, and so skinless is how I remain."

"H-how did you get in here?" Mum asked, ushering Sonny and Luna behind her. "Who are you?"

"Fantabulant questions, to which I have fantabulant answers! Firstly, I *let* myself in, which is child's play when you are me – which I am – for I have *these*." The skeleton wiggled his fingers and Luna noticed each bony digit ended in an equally bony key. "Second of all, my name is Keys ... Skeleton Keys. And though I always liked 'Bartholomew', I must admit my given name rather suits me." The skeleton abruptly held out his arm and gestured to his left. And *this* is my trusty assistant, Daisy."

"Where?" asked Dad. Skeleton Keys glanced sideways to see an empty space.

"Dogs 'n' cats, where has she gone?" he groaned. "She was here but a moment ago. This is the problem with a sidekick who can

39

turn invisible. Fret not! I am sure she will turn up..."

Luna peered at Skeleton Keys and suddenly felt as cold as she ever had – a gnashing cold that started in her bones and worked its way around her body. But she was quite sure it was not the sight of this walking, talking skeleton that chilled her blood. It was the portrait of Aunt Summer ... and that voice. Had she really heard her granddad, speaking to her from beyond the grave?

"Now then, I hope you frolicking fellow-me-folks will not give another thought to my appearance," Skeleton Keys continued. "For although I was once a figment of an overactive imagination, I am now your *best hope for survival.*"

"What do you mean?" asked Uncle Meriwether.

"I mean, you are all in terrible, terrible

danger!" Skeleton Keys exclaimed, flinging his arms into the air. "Possibly. I have not had a chance to look around. Tell me, has anything occurred of late that you might consider oddish or out of the ordinary?"

"I – I'm not sure what you mean," said Dad.

"We did just have a death in the family…" said Mum.

"Yes, there was that," said Dad.

"And we had a bit of a dance, we haven't done that before…" added Uncle Meriwether.

"True – that did make a nice change," said Dad.

"And Granddad came back as a ghost and turned Aunt Summer into a painting," said Luna.

"Yes," said Dad. "Granddad turned Aunt Summer into— *Wait, WHAT?*"

CHAPTER FOUR

THE TWITCH

(SOMEWHERE, THERE LURKS
AN UNIMAGINARY)

Times the Twitch Was Wrong: NEVER.
Apart from that one occasion ...
and that time with the flying cow...

A minute later Luna and her family (as well as the walking, talking skeleton with keys for fingers) were gathered around the portrait of Aunt Summer. The picture had shifted again – Aunt Summer was now holding out her arms, as if desperate for someone to reach into the painting and pull her out.

"Well, that *is* a flabbergaster," Skeleton Keys said, his skull cocked to one side as he peered at the portrait. "So you are saying that this painting appeared out of nowhere ... and now the young lady depicted in it is nowhere to be found?"

"Granddad turned Aunt Summer into a painting," repeated Luna. Simon Parker let out a nervous peep, as if in agreement.

"Cheese 'n' biscuits!" said Skeleton Keys. "That certainly puts the monkey among the bananas. However—"

"*However*, this is silly sausages, all in a string!" Dad cut in, jabbing his finger at the portrait. "That can't be Aunt Summer. She's got to be somewhere in the house. You can't put a person in a painting – it's not possible!"

"It is for a ghost," said Luna.

Mum turned to Luna and rested her hands on her shoulders.

"Sunbeam, that painting is just a painting," she said. "I'm sure there's a perfectly reasonable, reasonably perfect explanation for all this – Aunt Summer's probably just danced her way to the east wing. And we're certainly not being *haunted* ... except possibly by this skeleton man."

"'Tis true as turnips – there is no such thing as ghosts!" declared Skeleton Keys, whisking the painting off the wall. "What we are dealing with is *unimaginary*."

"Unimaginary?" repeated Mum. "Mr Keys, that is a made-up word."

"Are not *all* words made-up?" pondered Skeleton Keys. "My point is, some dallywanglers have *wild* imaginations. I should know – Ol' Mr Keys was once nothing more than an imaginary friend, until the day I was imagined so wildly and well that I became realer than earlobes! You mark my chin-wag, fellow-me-folks, somewhere in the shadows of this house there lurks an IF made real – an *unimaginary*."

Luna glared at Skeleton Keys. *Unimaginary?* she thought, the word repeating in her head.

But what about that voice? I know that voice...

"Imaginary friends coming to life?" Dad said. "You'll need a better excuse than that for breaking in and scaring the silly socks off everyone..."

"An excuse? I have the *twitch*!" replied Skeleton Keys proudly. "An uncanny rattle of the bones that lets me know when an imaginary friend has been *unimagined*," he continued. "The twitch is never wrong! Except that one time ... twice if you count the incident with the monster baby... Anyway, there I was, thinking important thoughts at home in my Doorminion, when every bone in my body had a sudden toothache. Lo and below, the twitch was upon me – an *unimagining* had occurred! And of all the infinite doors I could have opened, the twitch brought me here, to you."

"Sounds like a very tall story," said Mum with a raise of her eyebrow. "What would one of these unimaginary whatsits look like? Like you?"

"Like anything at all – imagination has no limits!" exclaimed Skeleton Keys. "But the truth of the fact is, one of *you* must have unimagined an IF."

"An IF?" repeated Dad.

"An imaginary friend! A companion of the mind," the skeleton replied, casting his gaze over each member of the family in turn. "Which of you did the unimagining? Think, dear dallywanglers..."

"I've never even had an imaginary friend," said Mum. "Never mind an *unimaginary* one."

"Neither have I," added Dad. "Silliness!"

"I'm starving," said Uncle Meriwether. "Anyone for cake?"

"I didn't do it!" blurted Sonny in a panic.

"And what about you, ankle-sprout?"
Skeleton Keys asked, leaning towards Luna
and glowering at the rat perched nervously
on her shoulder. "Perhaps only yesterday this
embiggened mouse was a figment of your
imagination..."

"Uh—" Luna began as Simon Parker darted
nervously into her pocket.

"Leave her alone," said Luna's dad, muscling in between Luna and the skeleton. "That rat is just a rat. Luna's had Simon Parker for *years*."

"Years? Hmm, that does spill ink on my theory," Skeleton Keys sighed.

"I don't need imaginary friends, I've got my family," Luna insisted as her rat crept back on to her shoulder. "Anyway, I heard my granddad's voice, and he isn't imaginary. He's dead."

"But who other than an unimaginary could have done *this*?" Skeleton Keys held up the painting. Aunt Summer's expression had changed again – she looked as if she was screaming. "I have seen an unimaginary turn to water in front of my very eye sockets ... another scoffed a bicycle in two bites ... one even conjured an actual pirate ship out of thin air. Conversion to canvas is quite conceivable."

"I don't want to get turned into a painting!" cried Sonny, running into his father's arms.

"It's all right, sunflower," added Mum matter-of-factly, before rounding on Skeleton Keys. "Instead of scaring my children, Mr Keys, why don't you help us find the actual Aunt Summer and we can put this behind us?"

"And then let us all meet in the kitchen for a slice of cake," suggested Uncle Meriwether with a chortle.

"Plantastic!" Skeleton Keys agreed, and slipped the portrait of Aunt Summer under his arm. "Oh, and do keep a look out for my trusty assistant, Daisy – she will be the one with the backwards head," he added. "Off we go then! First one to find an unimaginary wins!"

"We're looking for Aunt Summer!" snapped Dad.

"That too!" said Skeleton Keys.

CHAPTER FIVE

THE LIBRARY

(KEEP YOUR EYE SOCKETS PEELED)

The Moon family decided to split up and search the house for Aunt Summer. Haggard Hall was huge, with numerous corridors branching from one shadowy room to another – not to mention garages, stables and even a chapel, where Old Man Moon had just that morning been laid to rest. While Mum joined Uncle Meriwether to search the west wing, Luna and Sonny headed to the east wing with Dad and Skeleton Keys.

"Luna, do you really think Granddad came back ghostly?" whispered Sonny as they followed Skeleton Keys through one murky, bitterly cold corridor after another on their way to the east wing.

"I..." Luna began.

"You heard Mum, Sonny – that rotten old man is gone for good and is not the least bit ghostly," said Dad. "This is all a lot of silliness over nothing, isn't that right, Luna?"

Luna didn't reply. She wasn't sure she understood what was going on and she was certain her family didn't either. But there was one thing she *was* sure about – *she had heard her grandfather's voice.* And if anyone was going to keep their promise to come back as a ghost, it was Old Man Moon.

"You may rest assured, young sprouts, that nine and a half times out of ten, a haunting is simply an unimaginary friend making mischief," said Skeleton Keys.

"Mr Keys, would you *please* stop scaring the

children? There's no need to fill their heads with silly-sausage stories…" Dad said in a whisper. Then he fixed a grin to his face and turned to the children. "Everything's going to be great and groovy! Emergency hugs!"

"Emergency hugs!" Sonny repeated as Dad squeezed him tightly. Luna skirted around Dad and Sonny and picked up her pace until she reached a set of large double doors leading to the library. She grabbed both handles and swung open the doors. A fusty, dusty smell of unread books wafted up Luna's nose as they all made their way inside. The library had always been off-limits – Luna's grandfather claimed that reading produced big ideas … and big ideas were banned in Haggard Hall. The library became another secret for Luna to keep – only in the dead of night would she sneak inside and pore over the books, losing herself in facts, fictions and far-off worlds.

"When all this silliness is over we're going to read every book in here, and there's not a thing Old Man Moon can do about it," said Dad, giving Luna a wink. "We're going to read them all, out loud, and with all the funny voices. We'll turn down the corners of the pages and break the spines! Take that, you rotten old monster!"

"Dad, don't! Granddad'll *hear* you..." Luna whispered. She glanced over at Skeleton Keys, who leafed awkwardly through a book with key-tipped fingers, Aunt Summer's portrait still tucked under one arm. He seemed sure that this problem was caused by an 'unimaginary friend', which would mean Luna was wrong about her grandfather returning from the grave.

But I can't be wrong, Luna told herself. *I can't be...*

"Keep your eye sockets peeled, dallywanglers! There is an unimaginary around here somewhere, I can feel it in my bones…" said Skeleton Keys, searching under a nearby table. Simon Parker suddenly scuttled from Luna's shoulder up on to her head, emitting worried squeaks. Luna peered slowly upwards … and her jaw fell open. "We must be on the lookout for anything puzzling or perturbing," Skeleton Keys continued. "And that is not to say perplexing, peculiar or particularly petrifying…"

"L-like that?" Luna blurted. She pointed a trembling finger at the ceiling. Skeleton Keys looked up. The books, which had been neatly filed upon shelves just a moment ago, now floated in the air. Dozens upon dozens of books, suspended above their heads by some unseen force, their covers opening and closing like slow-beating wings.

"Crumcrinkles," said Skeleton Keys. "Fret not, ankle-sprouts! No harm can come from a good book..."

But little did Skeleton Keys know, these were not good books.

These books were BAD.

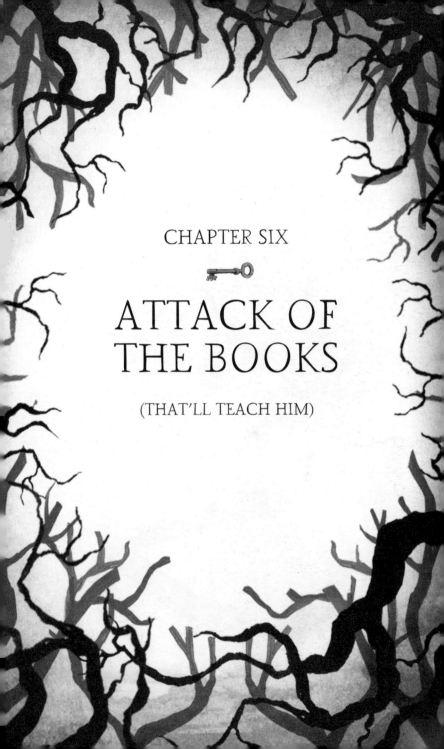

CHAPTER SIX

ATTACK OF
THE BOOKS

(THAT'LL TEACH HIM)

"Should you wish to take a look
Within the pages of a book
You'll find a world is waiting there
To whisk you off to who knows where!"
—SK

"Dogs 'n' cats!" Skeleton Keys cried as one of the flying books suddenly nosedived. The skeleton ducked as it whizzed over his head and slammed against a wall. "That is a turn-up for the books – these soaring stories are so bad they are positively unreadable!" he added. "They mean to do us a damage!"

The skeleton tried to make a break for the door, but it was immediately blocked by a seething mass of flapping books, which arced and wheeled in the air.

"B-but this is impossible!" uttered Dad, stunned into stillness. A moment later two more books swooped towards Sonny. Luna shrieked and pushed him out of the way – she felt the book part her hair as it flew overhead, missing Simon Parker by a literal whisker. It collided with the table before flapping dizzily back into the air. Then, as if the order had been given, more books began to dive, one after the other, flapping wildly.

"Watch out! Some of them are hardbacks!" howled Skeleton Keys as a flying book narrowly missed his skull. "Under the table, sprouts!"

Luna plucked her rat from her head and grabbed her brother by the arm. She dragged them under the table just as a dozen more books raced towards them. Sonny and Simon Parker both let out terrified squeaks as the books crashed on to the table with a deafening thud. The bigger books immediately returned to the air with awkward beats of their covers, while the smaller paperbacks flapped dazedly where they landed.

"Make it stop!" Sonny cried against the cacophony of noise, as he clung on to his sister for dear life.

"They're everywhere! *Do* something, Keys!" shouted Dad, desperately batting away the bombarding books.

"This would be the perfect time for my trusty assistant to do some trusty assisting..." grumbled Skeleton Keys. He held up one of his key-tipped fingers. "Fret not, for I wrote the book on exiting in style! Behold, *the Key to a Quick Getaway*! With this key I can create doorways where there are none, transporting us, as fast as the flash-bang of a whippadeedooo, from this place to another location entirely! It really is the most grinnering thing to behold. All I have to do is—"

"JUST DO IT!" screamed Dad.

"Ah, yes, perhaps a detailed explanation of the workings of my *wondiferous* digit must wait," Skeleton Keys continued. "I must find us an escape route before— UFF!"

A book suddenly struck the back of Skeleton Keys' head, sending him tumbling limply to the floor. The painting of Aunt Summer flew from his grasp and slid to a halt under the table. Aunt Summer seemed to stare at Luna from the painting, her face contorted in fear.

"Emergency hugs! Emergency hugs!" squealed a panicking Sonny.

"Dad! Help!" Luna cried.

"I'm coming!" shouted Dad. "I'm—"

An open book thumped him hard in the chest. He grabbed the book and tried to tug it away, but it pressed against him as if glued in place. Another book struck him, and a third and fourth, sending him tumbling backwards. Then every book in the room suddenly turned on him, and dived. Within seconds, Dad had disappeared – buried under a papery mountain.

Then, as swiftly as the attack began, it was over. The books were still. A deafening silence fell over the library as if the entire room had been shushed.

"Dad...? Dad!" Luna cried. She left Sonny huddled under the table and scrambled out. She hurried over to the mound of books and began digging through it. "Sonny, help me!"

By the time Sonny had plucked up the courage to help his sister, she was halfway through clearing the mountain.

"Where is he? Dad!" shouted Luna ... but a moment later she could see the library floor. Dad was nowhere to be seen. It was as if he had vanished.

"Where's he gone?" whimpered a trembling Sonny.

Simon Parker sniffed nervously at the last of the books, and its title jumped out at Luna:

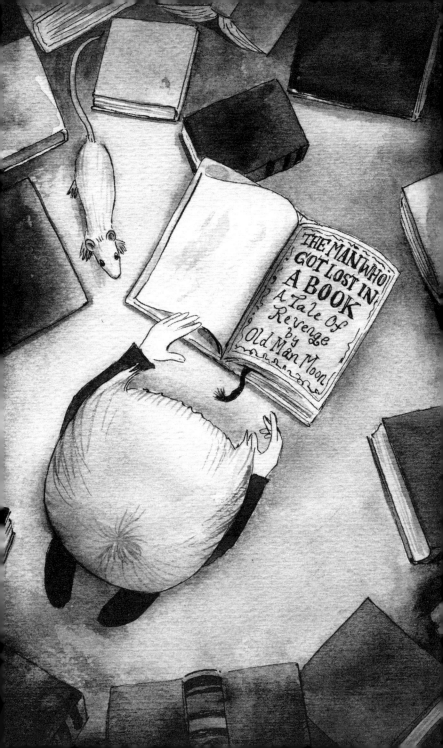

THE MAN WHO GOT LOST IN A BOOK

A Tale of Revenge
by Old Man Moon

"What…?" Luna muttered as she stared at the cover. She picked up the book and opened it at the first page.

"When all this silliness is over we're going to read every book in here, and there's not a thing Old Man Moon can do about it," said Dad, giving Luna a wink. "We're going to read them all, out loud, and with all the funny

voices. We'll turn down the corners of the pages and break the spines! Take that, you rotten old monster!"

But he didn't know that a ghost was haunting Haggard Hall.

Old Man Moon would make him pay.

Old Man Moon would make them all pay.

"That'll teach him," said a voice ... his voice.

"Sonny, did you hear that?" Luna asked. "Tell me you heard that..."

"Heard what? I didn't hear anything," replied Sonny with tears in his eyes. "Luna, where's Dad?"

"He – he's ... here," Luna whispered, holding the book tightly to her chest. "Granddad turned him into a book."

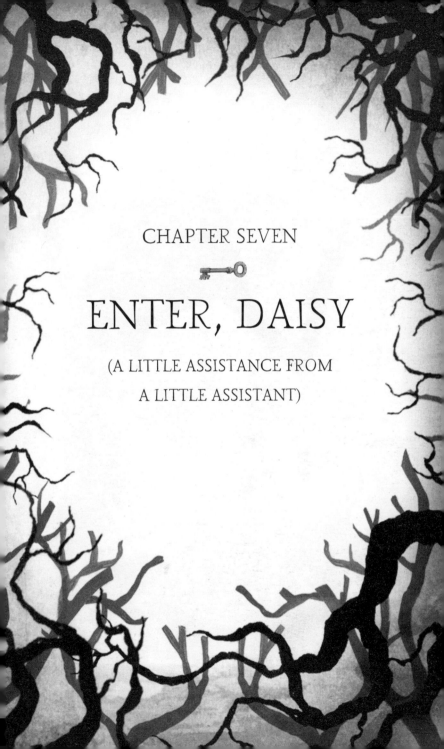

CHAPTER SEVEN

ENTER, DAISY

(A LITTLE ASSISTANCE FROM A LITTLE ASSISTANT)

From *The Important Thoughts of Mr S. Keys*
Volume 11: The Key to a Quick Getaway

Too dangerous to stop and stay?
Then use this key to get away!

"Crumcrinkles! I love a book that is full of surprises but that one nearly took my head off," groaned Skeleton Keys, rubbing his skull as he clambered to his feet. He looked round to see Luna and Sonny kneeling among hundreds of now lifeless books. "What luck! It appears our war with words is won. But tell me, where is your father?"

Luna got to her feet and held up the book in her hands.

"Granddad – he turned Dad into a book," she said as Sonny sobbed quietly. The skeleton carefully inspected the cover, his head slowly tilting from side to side.

"What a confuddling development!" confessed Skeleton Keys. "Transformed from man to manuscript – our mysterious unimaginary is quite the whizz at wizardry..."

"No, it's Granddad," said Luna firmly. "He did this. He's *haunting* us."

"B-b-b—" stuttered Sonny, his eyes wide with horror once again.

"*But* there is no such thing as ghosts. Quite right, Sonny!" said Skeleton Keys.

"B-b-b—" Sonny stammered again as Luna's rat let out a fearful squeak.

"But it *has* to be Granddad," insisted Luna, pointing to the book. "Look at the cover! His name is right there on—"

"B-BOOKS!" Sony screamed at last. Luna and the skeleton spun round. The books had taken to the air again, but this time they whirled and swirled in unison like a flock of starlings. Luna grabbed Simon Parker and secreted him back in her coat pocket as the books rose above them, preparing to strike.

"These books appear to be writing their own sequel!" said Skeleton Keys as the shadow of the book-flock fell over them.

"Hey!" came a cry. The flock whirled as one towards the sound. A girl appeared out of nowhere on top of the table. She looked to be around six but everything about her, from her skin to her pigtails to her striped dress, was grey, as if she belonged in a black and white photo.

And her head was on backwards.

"Daisy!" cried Skeleton Keys. "Finally a little assistance from my little—"

"I'm *not* your assistant," growled the girl with the backwards head.

"—partner! I was going to say partner,"

Skeleton Keys assured her. "And your distraction is most timely!"

"Distraction? Silly skeleton – I'm here to kick books and take names," Daisy grunted. She planted her feet on the table. "Come on then, you pathetic paperbacks. Fact or fiction, I'll pulp the lot of you."

With that, the books arced in the air as a single, great cloud and rounded on Daisy. The flock swooped up towards the ceiling before looming over her. But, even with nowhere to run, Daisy did not so much as flinch. Instead, she plucked a matchbox from her pocket, took out a match and lit it. A tiny, flickering flame burst into life.

Daisy raised the match above her head. The flock of books halted suddenly, their covers

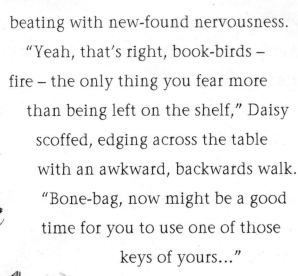

beating with new-found nervousness.
"Yeah, that's right, book-birds –
fire – the only thing you fear more
than being left on the shelf," Daisy
scoffed, edging across the table
with an awkward, backwards walk.
"Bone-bag, now might be a good
time for you to use one of those
keys of yours..."

"My what? Oh yes! I was just about to spring into action..." said Skeleton Keys. He thrust *the Key to a Quick Getaway* into a nearby wall and turned it with a CLICK CLUNK. In an instant and out of nowhere a doorway materialized in the wall. Skeleton Keys swung it open. "On the double, ankle-sprouts!"

With the book-that-was-once-Dad in one hand and Sonny's arm in the other, Luna dashed through the doorway. Skeleton Keys grabbed the painting of Aunt Summer from under the table and followed them through as Daisy hopped off the table with a smirk. She headed for the doorway, her backwards-facing head keeping a watchful eye on the books as her match burned slowly down.

"Any of you even turn a page and I'll—" she began, when Skeleton Keys appeared from the

doorway and

snuffed out

the flame

between two

fingers.

"Hey!"

Daisy snapped.

The flock of books immediately dived

towards them but Skeleton Keys was too fast

– he pulled Daisy through the doorway and

slammed the door shut behind them.

CHAPTER EIGHT

THE KITCHEN

(A PERFECTLY REASONABLE,
REASONABLY PERFECT EXPLANATION)

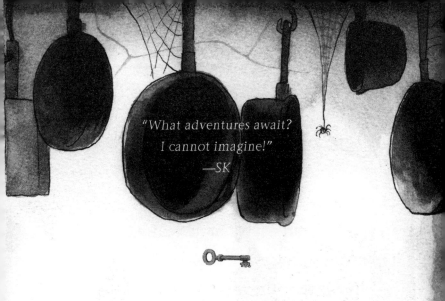

"What adventures await?
I cannot imagine!"
—SK

"You always spoil my fun, bone-bag," Daisy huffed as they emerged on the other side of the doorway.

"And you always give in to your more destructive impulses," replied Skeleton Keys. "You are more than the sum of emotions that led to your unimagining, Daisy … though for once, I am grateful you brought a box of matches."

Luna immediately realized that Skeleton Keys had, with the turn of a key, transported them all the way to the other side of the house. They were in the kitchen, just one dark corridor away from the great hall, where Aunt Summer had danced up the stairs into darkness. The room was square, drab and grey, with a large table in its centre and cupboards lining every wall.

"What is this, the *tenth* time I've saved your old bones?" Daisy scoffed as Skeleton Keys placed the portrait of Aunt Summer on the kitchen table. "I have literally no idea how you've survived this long without me."

Luna didn't realize she was staring at Daisy until the girl glowered back at her.

"What are you gawping at? Never seen a girl with a backwards head before?" she said, a strange, lopsided grin appearing on her face.

Luna quickly glanced away. She put the book formerly known as Dad on the kitchen table next to the painting and then checked on Simon Parker, encouraging him out of her pocket with soothing coos.

"I want Mum," Sonny whispered, tugging Luna's coat and sniffing tears up his nose. "Can I have an emergency hug? I'm scared..."

"You're always scared," Luna said softly. She gave Sonny a big hug and rubbed his back. "That's why you've got me."

"Why do you put up with him?" groaned Daisy. "He's wetter than a pair of wetted underpants."

"He's ... my brother. He needs me," said Luna.

"Well, if he was *my* brother I'd shake him by his feet 'til his crybaby tears made a puddle on the ground," said Daisy. "Then I'd push him over in it."

"That's a horrible thing to say," Luna said sternly.

"Thank you for noticing, sobby-socks," said

Daisy proudly. "Are you going to start crying now too?"

"I can't," Luna admitted flatly. "I don't know why, but the tears won't come out."

Daisy wasn't sure what to do with such an honest answer, so she just tutted and scuffed her feet on the floor.

"Dogs 'n' cats, Daisy, must you provoke every living soul you meet?" said Skeleton Keys, inspecting the book of Dad as it sat on the table.

"Making crybabies cry is my second favourite thing in life, after annoying you," replied Daisy. "Can we go home now? This whole place smells like old people."

"Not until we get to the bottom of the mysterious menace that plagues this family," replied Skeleton Keys. "Whatever lurks in the shadows of this house, it is making us look like a prize pair of saddle-geese."

"What do you think I've been doing all

this time?" Daisy huffed. "While you were playing happy families with this lot, I turned invisible and did what Daisy does – I searched the whole house looking for clues ... and anything worth nicking." With that, she pulled open one of the cupboards to reveal dozens of identical tins of soup. "Which, unless you really like soup, there isn't."

"Granddad didn't believe in chewing,"
explained Luna. "He said it made eating too
interesting."

"I wasn't talking to you, rat-shoulder,"
Daisy snarled. "Still, maybe you can explain
something to me. Most of the rooms are full
of nothing but dust. There aren't even enough
beds for everyone. Where do you all—"

"Luna! Sonny!"

Mum suddenly burst through the kitchen
door, with Uncle Meriwether hot on her
heels. Mum wasted no time in clutching Luna
and Sonny to her. "Oh, you two look like
you've seen a gho— I mean, are you all right?
Did you find Aunt Summer?"

"Mum! He got Dad!" Luna cried, grabbing
the book from the kitchen table. "Granddad
got Dad, look!"

"A book?" Mum said.

"Look at the cover! Read it!" Luna howled,

so loudly that Simon Parker let out a startled peep. "It's Dad … Granddad turned him into a book."

"Turned him into— Oh, sunbeam, that's just not possible," tutted Mum, taking the book from Luna. She looked at the cover and, despite her healthy glow, went rather pale. "I'm sure there's a perfectly reasonable, reasonably perfect explanation for all this," she said at last. "This is no more your father than that portrait is your aunt Summer – this is all a trick. An elaborate trick, but a trick nonetheless."

"Ugh, these dummies wouldn't know an unimaginary if it bit them on the bum, which it still might," tutted Daisy. "Come on bone-bag. Let's leave 'em to get turned into a pair of curtains or whatever."

"And who might you be?" said Mum, rounding on Daisy.

"I might be the Easter Bunny ... or I might be your worst enemy," Daisy replied, matter-of-factly. "Do you want to find out which?"

"This is my faithful-if-unmannerly partner-in-problem-solving, Daisy," interrupted Skeleton Keys. "Now, since you appear to be being picked off one by one, I suggest we all remain in this room until I can solve this mystery."

"Stay in the kitchen? Now you're talking!" said Uncle Meriwether with a nervous chuckle. "Why, this is where all the cakes are – and I for one am starving!"

"Cakes? Fat chance," Daisy scoffed.

"I beg your pardon?" said Uncle Meriwether.

"There's no cake for miles – just old man's soup as far as the eye can see," Daisy huffed, opening another cupboard and jabbing a finger at the numerous soup tins.

"But I always have cake! Scrumptious and melt-in-the-mouth moist, with a fresh layer of sweet icing!" chortled Uncle Meriwether, inspecting yet more soup-filled cupboards. "I wonder what can have happened to them? Why, I'll bet Dad and Aunt Summer are off scoffing 'em in secret, the tinkers!"

"They're not eating cake!" Luna snapped. "They're gone! Granddad has turned them into paintings and books and they're gone!"

"Fret not, ankle-sprout," said Skeleton Keys. "I will not leave until your peculiarly perplexing predicament is put to rights. You can trust Ol' Mr Keys to save the day..."

"*Can* we trust you?" snapped Mum. "You couldn't save my husband – what if you can't save the day?"

"Why, day saving is what I do! Apart from that one time ... twice if you count the incident with *you-know-who-you-do-*

not-know," mused Skeleton Keys. Then he scratched his skull and added grimly, "But today I *must* not fail. For if I do, you will continue to lose family members. One by one … until there is no one left."

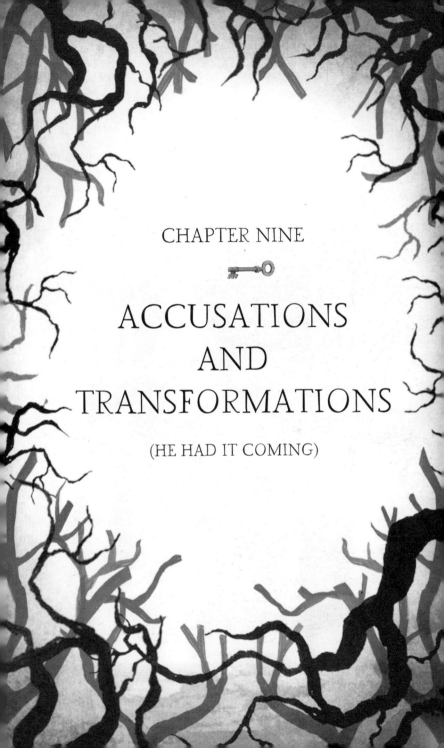

CHAPTER NINE

ACCUSATIONS AND TRANSFORMATIONS

(HE HAD IT COMING)

"Spirits and spectres, ghosts and ghouls
May spook a trembling mind
But if you look a little closer,
Unimaginaries, you find!"
—SK

"He won't stop," said Luna, her dark, sleepless eyes wide with fear. She looked at Mum, Sonny and Uncle Meriwether in turn. "Granddad won't stop haunting us until you're all gone."

"Flabberjabs," said Skeleton Keys. "There is clearly a simpler – or possibly infinitely more complicated – explanation. Perhaps, since we have yet to encounter an unimaginary, it can somehow render itself un-seeable, much like Daisy here..."

"It'd better not," said Daisy, disappearing

and reappearing in an instant. "Turning invisible is *my* thing."

"While we're on the subject of unimaginaries," said Mum, eyeballing Skeleton Keys, "all of this strangeness started happening around the same time *you* showed up – uninvited, I might add – to our house. How do we know you're not just playing a cruel game with us?"

"A game? Madam, I will have you know the only game I play is Operation," replied Skeleton Keys. "And I would not be here at all if one of you had not unimagined whatever mysterious figment of an overactive imagination now plagues this house..."

"Well, whatever you're going to do, I wish you'd hurry up about it – I'm *so* hungry!" Uncle Meriwether guffawed as he slapped his stomach. "I need cake, or I shall wither away to nothing!"

"Hat 'n' gloves, we really must focus on the matter in key-fingered hand," insisted Skeleton Keys. "I will not stand by and let this family fall! You are all under the protection of Skeleton Keys – Mum, ankle-sprouts and tiny Uncle Meriwether here..."

"*Tiny?*" scoffed Daisy. "Uncle cake-face is so big his belly button gets home before he ... does..."

Daisy trailed off as everyone turned to look at Uncle Meriwether.

"Oh *no*," Luna whimpered in horror as Simon Parker chirped frantically on her shoulder. "Not again..."

"What are you all staring at?" asked Uncle Meriwether with a nervous laugh. "Do – do I have cake stuck in my beard?"

"Uncle Meriwether, where are you going?" howled Sonny. Uncle Meriwether looked down to see the floor, suddenly closer than before. Then he spotted his feet instead of his round belly, which was getting smaller by the second. He glanced at his hands, and found his fingers were suddenly as thin as pencils.

Uncle Meriwether was shrinking in all directions. Shorter ... thinner ... smaller. His arms and legs drew into his body and within a few seconds he was so small that he was looking up at Sonny.

"What – what's happening to me?" he squeaked, his voice thin and high-pitched.

"Uncle Meriwether!" cried Mum, but it was too late. Uncle Meriwether continued to shrink and change, until with a desperate, "Don't eat all the caaaake..." his transformation was complete.

Uncle Meriwether had turned into a tin of soup.

There was a long moment of silence but for the nervous squeaking of Luna's rat from her shoulder.

"Crumcrinkles," said Skeleton Keys, plucking the tin off the floor. "Now we are really in the soup..."

"He *had it coming*," said that voice.

"No, not again!" Luna uttered, pacing around the room. "Stop, Granddad! Please, you have to stop!"

"Luna...? What is it?" asked Mum.

"You didn't hear him? You had to have heard him!" said Luna. "Granddad, don't send them away, please!"

"Luna, it's ... going to be all right," said Mum, but for once, she did not sound convinced. "I-I'm sure there's a perfectly reasonable, reasonably perfect explanation for—"

"There isn't!" Luna cried. "Why won't you believe me? It's Granddad! You all had so much fun at his funeral, all the laughing and singing and dancing and ... this is his revenge. He won't stop until he's got revenge on all of you. Not unless I stop him..."

Luna bolted for the door with such ferocity

that Simon Parker fell from her shoulder on to the table. Mum called, "Luna, wait!" but it was too late – Luna was gone.

Hello again, dallywanglers! Sorry to barge in like a monkey with a trumpet but I just wanted to make sure that you were not too terrified by the tale I have come to call *The Haunting of Luna Moon*. Of course, a few spine-chills and teeth-chatters can be good for the constitution, but I would not want any of you to be making puddles in your undergarments. Seeing a fellow transmogrified into a tin can may send even the soundest mind aquiver. At least that handsome, key-fingered skeleton is on hand to save the day. I am sure you will agree he is quite the heroic and finely dressed good-do-well...

Anyway, our terrifying tale is halfway told and events, if memory serves, are about to take an even more troubling turn. Luna Moon is convinced that the ghost of her grandfather is haunting her, determined to wreak terrible revenge upon the family for celebrating his demise. Luna's aunt has been transformed into a painting ... her father into a book ... and lo and below, Uncle Meriwether has just been turned into a tin of soup!

Now Luna flees into darkness, possessed by a single thought – she must convince the ghost of her grandfather to spare her family.

But Ol' Mr Keys is here to tell you what I told the young ankle-sprout – there are no such things as ghosts. Next time you hear tell of a spectre or spirit, monster, werewolf, vampire or bogie man I will show you the overactive imagination that started it all. Creatures from another world ... things that bump-a-dump in the night ... supernatural or just plain unnatural ... everything unimaginable is unimaginary. And I would not have it any other way!

Where was I? Oh yes! The mystery of Luna

Moon's haunting may be about to unfold.
This tale has secrets yet to be revealed and,
like a fish with a false moustache, all may not
be as it seems. That which we imagine to be
real may be but a figment of an overactive
imagination. And that which we imagine to
be a figment of the imagination may be very
real indeed...

For, as I think I might have mentioned,
strange things can happen when imaginations
run wild...

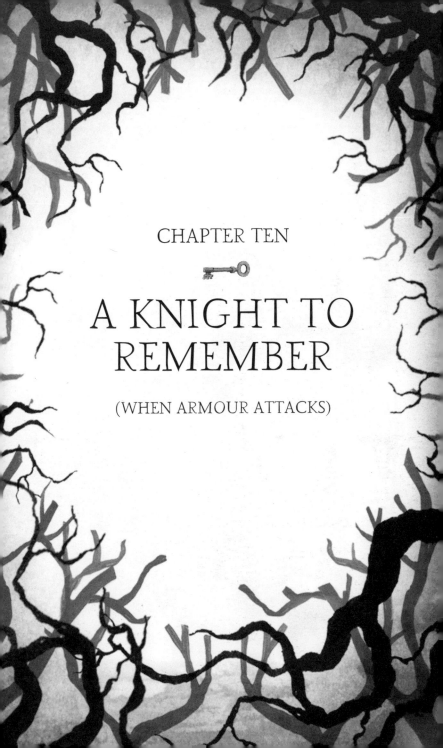

CHAPTER TEN

A KNIGHT TO REMEMBER

(WHEN ARMOUR ATTACKS)

"The pen is writier than the sword!"
—SK

"Luna! Come back!" shouted Mum.
Sonny called out too – even Simon
Parker let out a nervous squeak as Luna raced
out of the kitchen.

"M-Mum, I don't want to be turned into
soup," Sonny sobbed, cradling Luna's rat as he
huddled on the kitchen floor. Mum wrapped
him in her arms and held him tightly.

"You won't be soup, sunflower. We're –
we're going to be OK," said Mum, sounding
less sure by the moment. She turned to
Skeleton Keys. "Mr Keys, you swore that my

family was your top priority. So please, bring my daughter back to me. And close the door after you so you don't let the cold in."

"Madam, I will not fail you. Stay here with the boy until I return," Skeleton Keys said, placing the tin of soup that was once Uncle Meriwether on the table next to the book and painting. "Come on, Daisy!"

"But ... ugh, *fine*," Daisy groaned, following the skeleton out of the kitchen. Mum locked the door behind them and huddled around the table with Sonny and Simon Parker as Skeleton Keys and Daisy headed down the corridor – the pair emerged in the great hall to find Luna making a beeline for the front door.

"Luna, wait!" cried Skeleton Keys, pursuing her down the hall.

"Do you know how hard it is to chase after someone when your head is on backwards?" Daisy moaned as she followed behind.

"You're in my bad books, Sally sad-face!"

"Leave me alone!" Luna cried. She had to find a way to stop her grandfather punishing any more of her family. Since all this madness began when the family danced on his grave, *that* would be where Luna would throw herself at the old man's mercy. If he would listen to her pleas anywhere, it would be—

"Urf!" Luna's train of thought came to an abrupt halt as her feet went from under her. She fell hard on to the unforgiving floor.

With an "Owwwww", Luna rolled on to her back and looked up. She was confronted with the sight of the suit of medieval armour, clutching its sword. She hadn't even noticed it as she ran past, but as she gazed up at it Luna saw that its right leg was jutting out, as if it had taken a step forwards.

Had she tripped on the suit of armour ... or had the armour tripped her up?

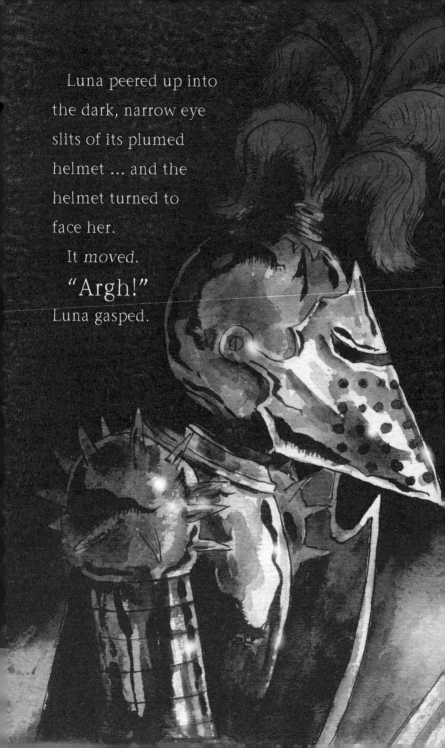

Luna peered up into the dark, narrow eye slits of its plumed helmet ... and the helmet turned to face her.

It *moved.*

"Argh!" Luna gasped.

Metal scraped against metal as the armour took a clanging step forwards. Then another step, and another. Luna scrambled backwards along the floor as, with a rusty creak, the suit of armour stamped towards her. She had no time to get to her feet before its dark shadow fell over her. Luna held her breath as the armour loomed
... and then
suddenly
turned
away.

Luna's breath puffed silently out of her mouth as she watched the armour wheel round to face Skeleton Keys and Daisy. It lifted its iron arms and raised its sword above its head, stomping towards them with ground-shaking steps.

It's not after me, Luna thought, *it's after them.*

"Look out!" she cried.

"Fret not, ankle-sprout, I have sworn to protect you!" said Skeleton Keys as the armour rounded on them. "By my bones, I will be your knight in shining arm—

AARGH!"

Skeleton Keys ducked as the armour swung its sword. The blade shaved a millimetre of bone from his skull before digging into the floorboards with a

SLUDD!

Daisy immediately turned invisible.

"Daisy, get back here this instant! This rampant rugslugger means to cut me down to size!" cried Skeleton Keys. He skidded between the suit of armour's iron legs and clambered up on to its back. With one hand, the skeleton grabbed its sword-clutching gauntlet and with the other he clung to the plume of its helmet. "Luna, run!" he yelled as the armour thrashed forwards and back, trying to shake him loose.

The armour swung its sword again, taking Skeleton Keys with it. The skeleton flew helplessly through the air, sailing over Luna's head before crashing to the ground with a bony clatter.

"Skeleton! Mr Keys!" Luna cried as she hurried over to the skeleton. She gingerly shook him by the shoulder but the skeleton just rattled limply. Luna glanced back. The armour was striding towards them with heavy, metallic strides, its sword held aloft.

Luna closed her eyes and hoped for a miracle.

Instead she got a girl with a backwards head.

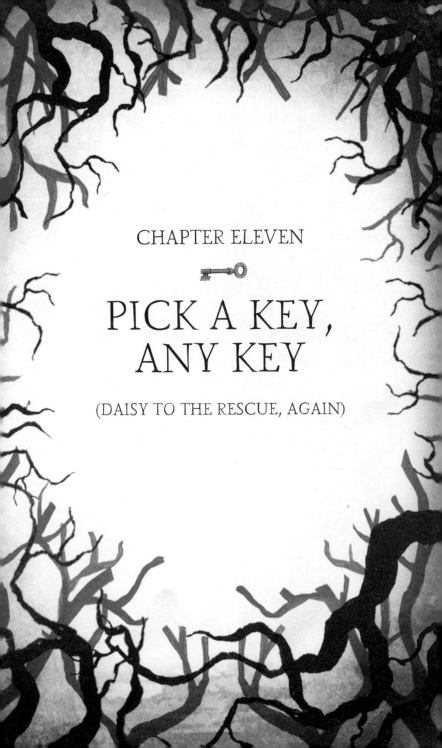

CHAPTER ELEVEN

PICK A KEY, ANY KEY

(DAISY TO THE RESCUE, AGAIN)

"It is gladdening to have a friend.
But it is useful to have a Daisy."
—SK

"Hey, rusty! Over here!" cried a voice.

As the suit of armour wheeled round, Daisy materialized at the far end of the hall. "I've seen bigger swords in a toyshop – you couldn't cut *butter* with that thing."

The armour stomped down the hall towards Daisy, swinging its sword wildly, but the moment it got within slicing distance, a lopsided grin spread across Daisy's face.

"Now you see me, now you don't," she said, before vanishing into thin air. Luna reached over Skeleton Keys, grabbed hold of the front door handle and pulled herself to her feet. With one eye on the suit of armour clanking around in search of Daisy, she turned the handle ... but the door would not open.

"Locked...!" Luna whimpered, glancing frantically around. "No, no, no..."

"Looking for a key?" whispered Daisy, suddenly appearing by her side. She slapped a hand over Luna's mouth to stifle the shriek that escaped. "Lucky for you, I always keep a few spares lying around."

Daisy reached down to Skeleton Keys' limp body and lifted his left arm.

"Pick a key, any key," she said, grabbing the skeleton's thumb and jamming it into the lock.

"Hurry...!" whispered Luna. Daisy let out a tut before turning the key with a loud *CLICK CLUNK*. The sound echoed across the hall ... and the armour whirled round to face them.

"Oops," Daisy added with a smirk.

"Whuuutshappening...?" mumbled a dazed Skeleton Keys, his words slurring through his teeth. "Whatareyoudoingwithmykeyyys?"

"On your feet, bone-brain, or I'm leaving you behind," Daisy instructed as the armour began striding towards them. She glowered at Luna. "What are you waiting for, a written invitation? *Open the door.*"

"Sorry!" Luna turned the handle and yanked the door open. Bright, hazy light streamed in from outside, blinding her for a moment. As her eyes adjusted, Luna squinted at the snow-covered hill, then up at the blue sky. Somehow, the sun was shining outside, even though it was the dead of night inside the house.

"*How...?*" Luna muttered.

"Who cares? *Move,*" ordered Daisy. She shoved Luna out into the snow and then dragged Skeleton Keys through the door by his arm. Luna glanced back to see the armour raise its sword once more. She shrieked and pulled the door to close it, when:

SHUNK!

The armour's sword drove through the thick wood, the gleaming tip of the blade stopping a fraction short of Luna's nose.

"Time to run, dummies," said Daisy. There was no debate. As the suit of armour tried to prise its sword free, Luna and Daisy ran. They each took one of Skeleton Keys' bony arms and dragged him through the thick, falling snow. "On your feet, you bag of bones," Daisy insisted, elbowing him in the side of the head. "Unless you want Sir Chopsalot to divide you up into itty-bitty bony bits.

"How – oww – long have I been
insensible?" Skeleton Keys groaned, coming
to. "What is happening?"

"We're horribly out of our depth and
running for our lives. So same old, same old,"
Daisy replied as Skeleton Keys got to his feet.

They picked up the pace. Luna's breath
escaped her mouth in urgent clouds. She
wondered how far she could run. The grounds
of Haggard Hall stretched in every direction
and the forest of dead trees ahead of them
wasn't much of a hiding place. Then, as the
muscles in her legs started to burn from effort,

she dared to look back at the house, and saw
the armour tear its sword out of the door.

"It's coming!" Luna cried as the armour
began stomping tirelessly after them, its
sword brandished and ready.

"Better find a place to hide then,
Glumbelina, 'cause that medieval monster's
not going to stop until we're all deader than
your old granddad," said Daisy.

"Wait, the chapel! That's where I was
going!" said Luna. She pointed left up a steep
hill to the peaked spire of the small, stone
chapel. "We can hide in there!"

"A much better prospect than outpacing that metal monstrosity," said Skeleton Keys. "Lead the way, ankle-sprout – our time is running out!"

CHAPTER TWELVE

THE KEY TO REALITY

(RACE TO THE CHAPEL)

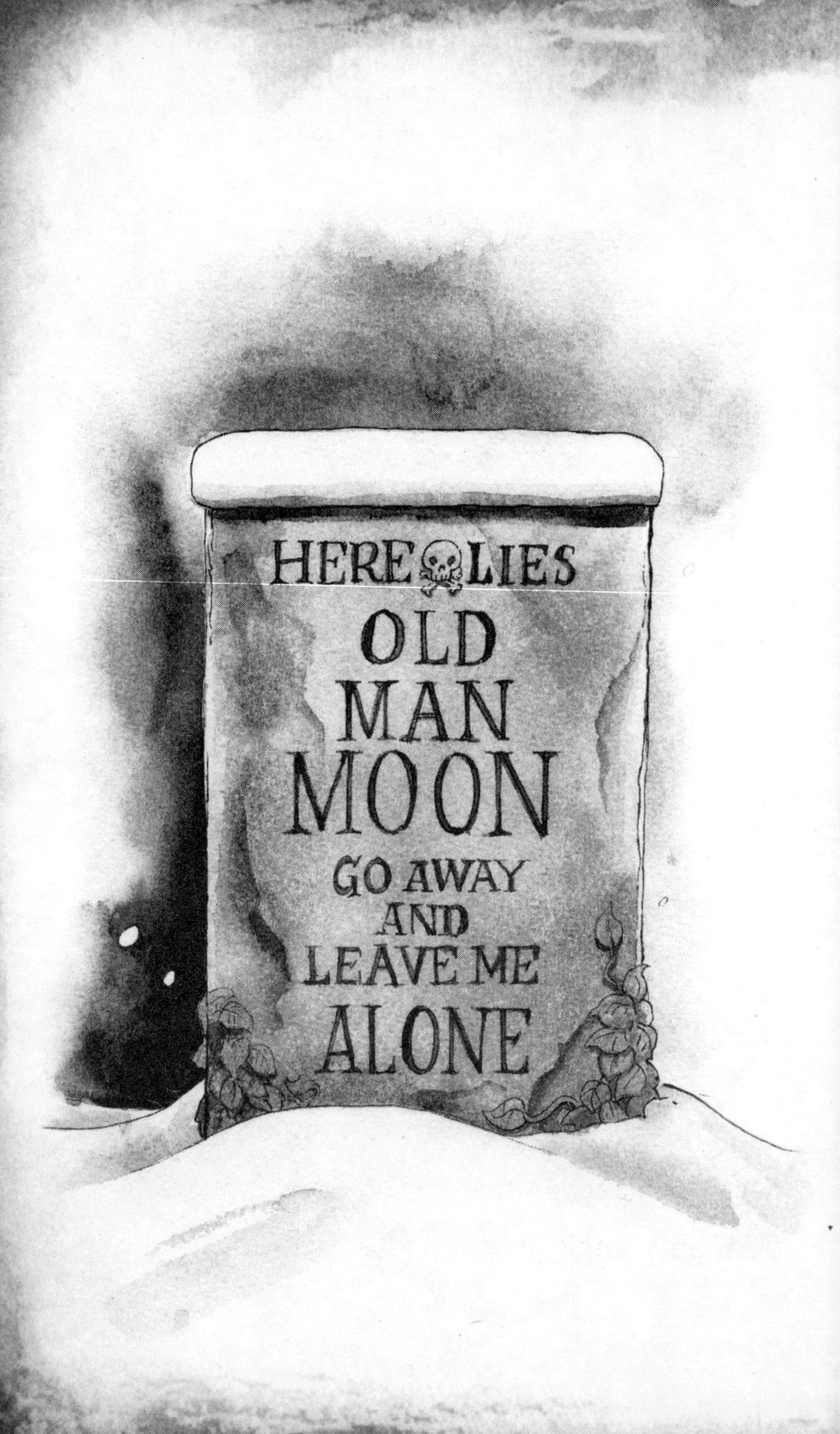
HERE LIES
OLD
MAN
MOON
GO AWAY
AND
LEAVE ME
ALONE

Realities To Avoid:
The World to End All Worlds
The World Where Hedgehogs are Evil
Backwards Goes That World The
The World Where Everything Happens Twice
The World Where Everything Happens Twice

"Faster, lest diddle-dallying proves deadly!" cried Skeleton Keys as the trio raced through the sock-freezing snow past dark, twisting trees and up the hill towards the chapel. As she ran, Luna's mind raced far faster than her legs. The past few hours had felt like a strange dream but one thought remained clear – her grandfather would not stop unless she stopped him.

The suit of amour was gaining on them fast as they reached the chapel. In its graveyard stood a single gravestone, which read:

HERE LIES
OLD MAN MOON
"GO AWAY AND LEAVE ME
ALONE"

I'll be back, Granddad.:. Luna thought as
she hurried by. *We need to talk.*

She dared to glance behind her one last time.
The armour was now only a few steps away.

"Fret not, I have a key for every occasion,"
insisted Skeleton Keys as he steadied himself
against the chapel door. He took a moment
to inspect his fingers in turn. "But which one
should I choose? *The Key to Possibility?* No,
too unpredictable... *The Key to Oblivion?*
Bread 'n' butter, not after last time..."

"*Pick one,* bone-bag," snapped Daisy.

"Aha! *The Key to Reality!* This one is a hum-
dum-dinger – it opens a doorway to any one of
an infinite number of *alternate realities.* Worlds
like our very own ... but flabbergastingly

different! The World Where It Never Stops Raining ... The World Where Everyone Talks Backwards ... The World Where No One Has Teeth ... The World Where—"

"Just *do* it!" Daisy growled, turning invisible as the armour loomed over them. Skeleton Keys quickly slipped a finger into the door's lock and turned the key with a *CLICK CLUNK*. Then, as the armour went to strike, the skeleton swung open the chapel door.

"BLOOAR!"

Skeleton Keys ducked as a tentacle shot out of the door. It was as wide as a tree trunk and a glowing, greenish colour, while its underside was covered with a hundred pulsating yellow suckers. The tentacle wrapped around the armour and gripped it tightly. The armour thrashed and squirmed, pounding the monstrous appendage with its iron gauntlets.

A moment later the tentacled monster dragged the armour back through the doorway with such speed that it seemed to disappear.

"Perfect," said the skeleton. "The World Where Absolutely Everything Is a Monster."

Luna dared to peek around the doorway and saw that the tentacle belonged to an oval, green-scaled monster as big as a double-decker bus and with far more giant limbs than it knew what to do with.

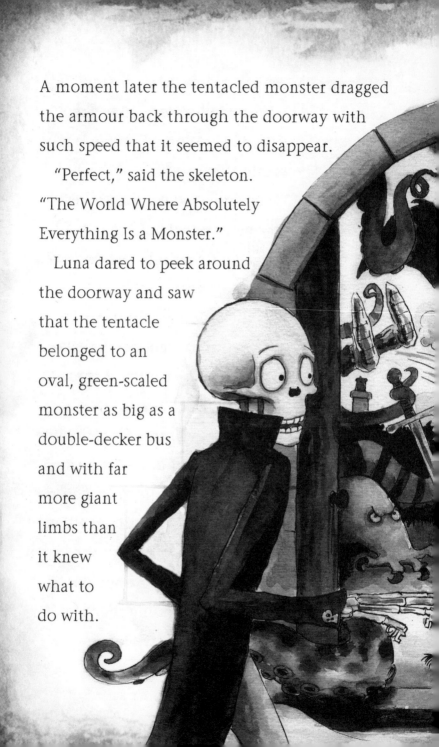

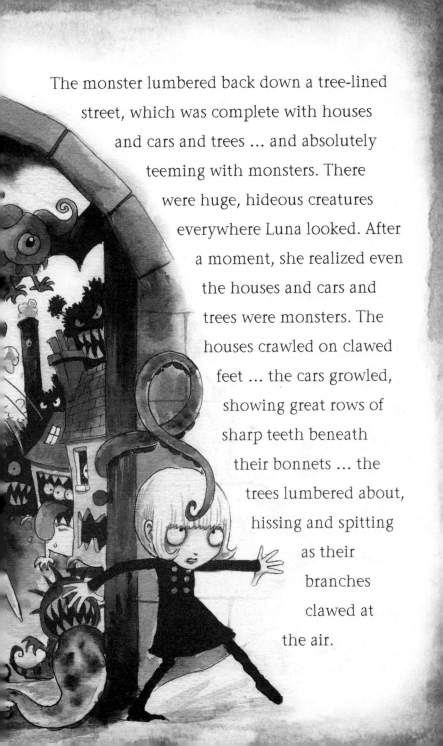

The monster lumbered back down a tree-lined street, which was complete with houses and cars and trees … and absolutely teeming with monsters. There were huge, hideous creatures everywhere Luna looked. After a moment, she realized even the houses and cars and trees were monsters. The houses crawled on clawed feet … the cars growled, showing great rows of sharp teeth beneath their bonnets … the trees lumbered about, hissing and spitting as their branches clawed at the air.

"Everything's monsters..." Luna whispered.

"*Absolutely* everything," replied Skeleton Keys.

"Looks like fun," said Daisy, reappearing to look through the door. "Let's get in there and make trouble."

"Not a chance – you cause quite enough huff 'n' hubbub in this reality," replied Skeleton Keys, slamming the door shut. With another *CLICK CLUNK* of the lock, the door once again became nothing more than a door. "Now, we must return Luna to her mother as soonish as possible and prevent— Crumcrinkles, I have just realized the sun is out! Was I insensible for an entire day?"

"Not my fault," replied Daisy. "It was your thumb that did it."

"My thumb? Which thumb?" asked the skeleton, sticking his left thumb in the air. "Not *this* thumb?"

"Stop saying 'thumb'," snarled Daisy. "But yes, I suppose it might have been that thumb."

"Cheese 'n' biscuits!" said Skeleton Keys, inspecting his digit with a tilt of his head. "This is *the Key to Time*."

"The what?" Daisy asked, eyeing the thumb suspiciously. "Wait a minute, you told me that one was the key to your room full of old pencils..."

"Ah, yes," Skeleton Keys said, scratching the back of his skull sheepishly. "The truth is, there is no room of old pencils – although I would dearly like one. I just told you that because if you knew about *the Key to Time* you would almost certainly have knocked off my head and stolen it for some unkindly, self-serving plot."

"And after we're finished here, that's exactly what I'll be doing," Daisy sneered as

Luna glanced back down the hill towards the house. The sunlight had slowly begun to fade, casting a reddish glow over the shimmering snow. She noticed a figure trudging slowly up the hill towards them. Was it Mum? Sonny? Luna squinted in the fading light as the figure came closer. It was a pale-looking girl of around nine years old, dressed from head to toe in black, but with a sharp bob of pure white hair. And upon her shoulder sat an equally white rat.

Luna's jaw fell open.

"Is that...?" she began, pointing a trembling finger. "Is that me?"

Skeleton Keys craned his whole body down the hill, and held a bony hand over his eye sockets.

"That is indeed you," he replied. "But it is the you that was ... the beforehand you ... the Luna Moon that has already been you."

"What do you mean?" Luna asked.

"I mean that we are no longer when we were," Skeleton Keys replied. "We have travelled back in time."

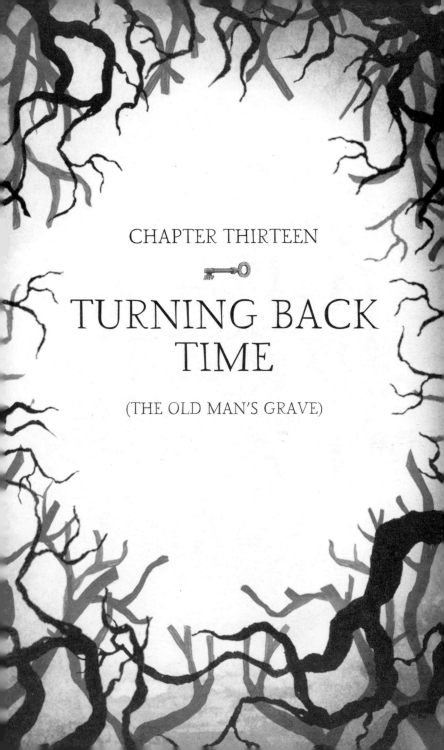

CHAPTER THIRTEEN

TURNING BACK TIME

(THE OLD MAN'S GRAVE)

There is a knack to handling time
So if in doubt, just check this rhyme.
With careful caution turn this key
In case you mess up history!

"Back in time?" groaned Daisy as they watched Luna's past self trudge through the snow towards the chapel. "Ugh, does that mean I have to rescue you two babies all over again?"

"*The Key to Time* opens a doorway to the past – when Daisy used the key to escape the house, she must have transported us back in time," explained Skeleton Keys. "We simply cannot risk Luna meeting her past self – it could result in complete cosmic catastrophe, tearing the very fabric of space-time asunder and bringing an end to the universe as we know it! Or so I am told."

"The end of the universe?" said Daisy. "Now that I'd like to see."

"There is no time to waste, pun intentional," continued Skeleton Keys. "Into the chapel, dallywanglers!"

The three of them hurried inside. The sight of the small stone room, with its uncomfortable rows of wooden pews, immediately took Luna back to earlier that day, when she had attended her grandfather's funeral. Just as Old Man Moon predicted, nobody came to pay their respects. The old man had been as hated in death as he was in life. No one had shed a single tear.

Luna gazed out of the window to the left of the chapel door, with Skeleton Keys peering over her shoulder. Daisy, who was too short to look out of the window, sat on a pew and grumbled.

"It's really me ... I mean, it was," said Luna, watching her past self stop at her granddad's gravestone and slump to her knees in the snow. "This happened a few hours ago. I went back to the grave to say goodbye. I didn't want to be alone..."

Skeleton Keys edged away from the window, feeling oddly guilty about witnessing Luna's moment of mourning.

"Poor ankle-sprout," Skeleton Keys whispered to Daisy. "Old Man Moon may have been a bad-hearted beetle-back, but he was still her grandfather. She must have felt so terribly— Wait, did she say 'alone'?" Skeleton Keys said, spinning on his heel to face Luna. "Forgive me sticking my elbow in upon your mournful moment, but why would you be *alone?*" the skeleton asked. "What about the rest of your family? Where are— Urrgh!"

"Now what?" asked Daisy impatiently.

"'Tis the twitch!" Skeleton Keys replied, the sensation suddenly rattling every bone in his body. "This one is a hum-dum-dinger! I have not felt a twitch so itchy-twitchy since – well, since this afternoon, when it brought me to Haggard Hall..."

As Skeleton Keys tried to get his twitch under control, he glanced out of the window again and saw the air around Luna's past self become hazy with shimmering light.

"I remember ... I was thinking about family," said Luna as she stared through the chapel window, watching her own past repeat itself. "I – I was *imagining*..."

Then, from out of thin air, appeared a woman dressed all in white, with blond hair, golden-tanned skin and kind eyes.

It was Mum.

A moment later another figure materialized – a man, dressed in a white jumper and trousers, with broad shoulders and a sensible haircut.

Dad.

A moment later, Aunt Summer appeared out of nowhere, closely followed by Uncle

Meriwether ... and finally, little Sonny.

"Horse 'n' cart, it cannot be!" Skeleton Keys gasped as his twitch threatened to shake him to pieces. "Luna Moon, your whole family is *unimaginary*."

CHAPTER FOURTEEN

LUNA'S UNIMAGINARY FAMILY

(BACK TO THE PRESENT)

From *The Important Thoughts of Mr S. Keys,*
Volume 1: The Key to Time
The First Rule of Time Travel
(Incorporating Time Travel Rules 2 to 11)

NEVER BUMP INTO YOUR OWN PAST

"I knew it!" exclaimed Daisy, shoving past Luna. She hopped up and down to get a look out of the window and saw Luna's past self gasp and spin round to see the five newly unimagined IFs gathered around her. "That's why I could only find two beds in this horrible house! This little liar doesn't even have a family – she *unimagined* them."

"I'm not a liar!" Luna snapped. "You asked me if I had imaginary friends, not an imaginary family!"

"Dogs 'n' cats, an entire *family* of

unimaginaries," Skeleton Keys said in a reverie. "Mother, father, aunt, uncle and a little brother – straight from your imagination and as real as hats! I *knew* there was an unimaginary in Haggard Hall, but five, all unimagined at once? No wonder the twitch left me rattled..."

"So, let me get this straight," Daisy said, eyeballing Luna suspiciously. "Before this afternoon – before you imagined yourself a mum and dad and that little annoying one and the rest, it was just you and the old man rattling around that grotty old house?"

"Granddad brought me up," confessed Luna, watching through the window as her past self hugged each of her 'family' in turn. "But he was never nice to me, so I imagined there were people who were. I imagined a family. They were kind and caring and thoughtful, and they never told me to go or get out or leave them alone ... oh, and they hated Granddad. But they weren't real. Not until..."

"Not until you unimagined them this afternoon, after your grandfather's funeral," said Skeleton Keys softly. "You poor sprout – you must have felt so terribly lonely."

"You're missing the point, bone-bag," snarled Daisy, squaring up to Luna. "Why didn't Sally sad-face here tell us that her whole family was a figment of her imagination? Why didn't *they* say anything? Bunch of sneaky, timewasting—"

"They don't know!" Luna blurted. "I mean, I don't think they know I imagined them..."

"Ah yes, the transition from imaginary to unimaginary can indeed be a confuddling affair – a newly unimagined IF may very well imagine that they have *always* been real," explained Skeleton Keys.

"I was going to tell them but then I didn't want them to think they weren't my real family," Luna said, peering out of the window again at her own past. "I *wanted* them to be real."

"Real for now, you mean," scoffed Daisy. "Most of them don't even last the night..."

"Daisy!" Skeleton Keys snapped.

"Wait, that's it ... that's it!" Luna said. "Dad, Aunt Summer, Uncle Meriwether – I can *change things* ... I can stop them dancing on Granddad's grave! Then Granddad won't come back and haunt us!"

"But do you not see, ankle-sprout? This *proves* there is no ghost," said Skeleton Keys. "Thanks to your wild imagination, Haggard Hall is brimming with unimaginaries. One of *them* must be responsible for this so-called haunting! Someone is playing a sneakish and sharp-hearted trick upon—"

"No! No, it is Granddad!" Luna shouted, making a dash for the chapel door. "I can stop him – I can stop it from happening!"

"Wait!" said Skeleton Keys, leaping in front of the door and throwing his arms out. "Luna, you must not encounter your past self! 'Never Bump Into Your Own Past' – it is the first rule of time travel! And rules two to eleven, for that matter. I am not qualified to put a shattered universe back together again!"

"Let me out!" Luna shouted. "You're wrong! Granddad came back!"

"Luna, I am sorry ... but I cannot," said Skeleton Keys. Then he slipped the *Key to Time* into the lock and turned.

CLICK
  CLUNK.

"No!" Luna cried. She pushed Skeleton Keys aside and pulled open the door. Luna's family and her past self had vanished. Instead she saw a night sky filled with stars and snowfall.

With the turn of a key, the skeleton had returned them to the present.

"Why did you do that?" Luna snapped, racing out into the biting air. She dragged herself through the snow to the gravestone. "I could have saved them!"

Skeleton Keys followed her out into the darkness.

"Luna, your grandfather is *not* responsible

for what's happening," he said. "Your grandfather is—"

"Don't say it! Don't say he's gone!" Luna screamed. "He can't be! He – he can't be gone…"

"What do you care if the old man's gone anyway?" tutted Daisy. "I thought you hated him."

"He was all I had!" Luna cried. She slumped to her knees again. The realization came to her in a cold wave of sadness – despite the old man's unkindness, despite every mean thing he ever said or did, he had brought her up and kept her safe. He was her family … and she was his. She would have done anything to bring him back.

"I really am sorry, sprout," Skeleton Keys said softly.

Luna peered up into the night sky. "Granddad brought me here, just once," she said. "It was the only time I ever saw him leave the house. He waited for the coldest night of the year. He took me through the snow to the top of the hill and he pointed up at the stars. He said, 'I don't like stars. Everyone thinks they're special, but stars are everywhere. There are more stars in the universe than specks of dust.' Then he pointed at the moon and he said, 'But you are the moon. There's only one of you'." Luna sniffed and stared up into the sky. "He was all I had ... but I was all he had too."

Then, at last, tears began to roll down Luna's cheeks. Within moments she was crying uncontrollably. Luna wept for her grandfather until she was exhausted, her warm tears peppering the fresh snow. She sobbed until no more tears would come.

"Crybaby," muttered Daisy out of the corner of her mouth. Skeleton Keys shushed her by placing a key-tipped finger to his teeth, and knelt beside Luna.

"Your grandfather may be gone, Luna, but we still have a chance to save your unimaginary family," he said. Luna wiped her nose with her sleeve and sniffed, twice.

"How?" she asked.

"I am glad you asked!" the skeleton replied. Then he scratched his head. "I have not the wisp of a clue."

"Are you sure you've been doing this two hundred years, bone-head?" tutted Daisy. "Face facts, there are only two suspects left – Mum and the other crybaby."

"Suspects?" Luna said. "But neither of them would have – *could* have done all this!"

"How do you know?" Daisy asked with a shrug.

"They're my family!" said Luna. "And I imagined them!"

"A well-brained fellow-me-chap told me that once you eliminate the impossible, whatever remains, no matter how *unimaginable*, must be the truth," said Skeleton Keys. "Although he also told me that horses cannot sneeze, which turns out to be a load of old—"

"HELP!"

The cry echoed up the hill from the house.

"Sonny?" Luna gasped, dragging herself to

her feet. "That's Sonny!"

"Sticks 'n' stones, the little ankle-sprout is in trouble!" Skeleton Keys cried. "Back to Haggard Hall, dallywanglers, *before we are too late*."

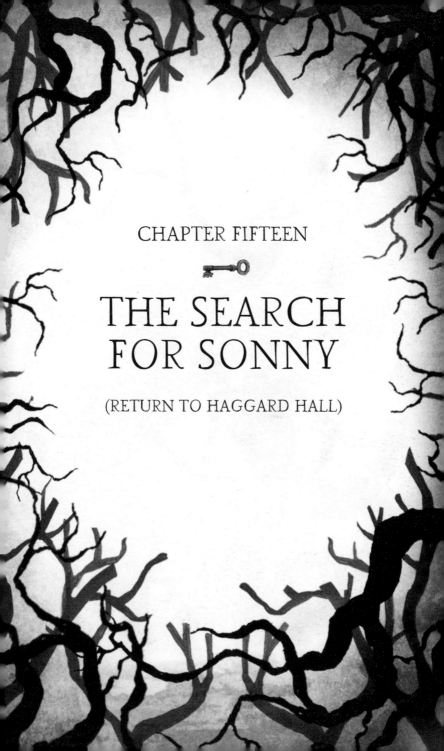

CHAPTER FIFTEEN

THE SEARCH FOR SONNY

(RETURN TO HAGGARD HALL)

From Ol' Mr Keys' Unimaginable Adventures, No. 48
– Journey to the Centre of the Middle

All doors are there for the opening!
Except those that are better off closed.

"HELP!"

Sonny's panicked cries grew louder as Luna and Skeleton Keys hurried back through the night towards Haggard Hall, with Daisy following behind.

"I wish someone would shut him up," Daisy muttered, her awkward backwards walk ever more awkward as she navigated the deep snow.

"Sonny! Hang on!" Luna shouted again as they reached the front door. She grabbed the handle but it wouldn't turn. "It's locked!" Luna cried.

Skeleton Keys ran a key-shaped finger down the door frame and felt ice crystals cracking beneath his touch. "Dogs 'n' cats, not locked ... this door is *frozen* shut."

"Looks like somebody let the cold in," said Daisy.

Skeleton Keys took two sidesteps and faced the wall.

"You have to try harder than that to stop Ol' Mr Keys – *the Key to a Quick Getaway* is good for entrances as well as exits," he said. With that, he thrust the key into the wall. With a *CLICK CLUNK* he turned the key and a door materialized in the wall. "Brace yourself, sprout – if Sonny is in peril, that means your unimaginary mother *must* be behind all this madness ... just as I always suspected," the skeleton added, swinging open the door and stepping through. "After all, the twitch is never— Ah."

"What is it?" Luna whispered, pushing past Skeleton Keys. Then, in the centre of the hall, she saw her.

Mum was standing in the middle of the floor, as still as a statue, her arms outstretched, her face fixed in a look of fright. She was a glimmering, bluish-white, and moonlight danced and sparkled over her whole body. Luna edged closer as the terrible reality of the situation dawned upon her.

Mum had been turned into ice.

"Crumcrinkles, we are too late – the phantom unimaginary has struck again!" Skeleton Keys cried. "The plot thickens!"

"Thickens? The plot couldn't be any *thinner*," said Daisy. "If Mum's been put on ice, the 'phantom unimaginary' must be the little brat, Sonny."

"Sonny, of course!" declared the skeleton. "Just as I always suspec—"

"HELP!"

Sonny's scream came from upstairs. Without stopping to think, Luna sped across the great hall and up the stairs.

"Wait! It could be a trap! A con-ploy! A sneakish swindling!" Skeleton Keys cried after her. But Luna did not wait. She sped to the top of the stairs and rounded the corner. She followed Sonny's cries across the night-black landing, turning another corner, before suddenly skidding to a halt. A shiver ran down Luna's spine as she realized where she'd ended up.

"The horridor," she said aloud. She peered up to see the glaring, judgmental stares of her grandfather's portraits.

"HELP!" came Sonny's cry from inside her grandfather's room.

"Sonny! I'm coming!" Luna cried, but before she could take another step a pair of arms reached out of the nearest painting and grasped at her. Luna howled in shock. As she squirmed free, she could see the portrait of her grandfather starting to drag itself out of the frame. And this strange, painted ghost was not alone. More portraits came to life, reaching out of their frames and clawing at the air, creating a gauntlet of ghostly grandfathers.

"You're not my granddad ... none of you are. He's gone. Granddad's gone!" Luna said.

She clenched her fists and gritted her teeth. "I'm coming, Sonny!"

With her heartbeat thumping in her ears, Luna put her head down, shut her eyes and raced as fast as she could down the horridor. She did not stop running until she ran straight into the door of her grandfather's room. She grabbed the handle and swung it open.

"Uff!" Luna grunted as she fell to the floor. With her head spinning, she opened her eyes. The first thing she saw was her rat, staring at her through beady black eyes, his nose twitching nervously.

"Simon – *oww* – Parker?" said Luna, smiling with relief. She dragged herself on to her knees as the rat scuttled on to her shoulder. She stroked his head and he let out a happy chirrup. "What happened? Where's Sonny?"

Simon Parker twitched his whiskers unhelpfully.

Luna looked around. Her granddad's cavernous bedroom was as dark and dreadful as ever, with only a few slivers of pale moonlight streaking through threadbare curtains to illuminate a four-poster bed. It took Luna a moment to adjust to the deeper darkness ... and then she saw it.

There was something under the bed.

No, not something.

Someone.

"L-Luna?" whispered the someone. "Emergency hug..."

"Sonny!" Luna cried. Sonny was curled in a ball and shivering under the bed, his bright, tearful eyes glinting with fear. "Are you all right? What's going on? What happened to Mum?"

"H-he got her ... he turned her into ice!" Sonny whispered in fear. "Th-then he came after *me*."

"Who did?" Luna asked, pulling herself to her feet. "Who came after you?"

"H-him...!" whimpered Sonny, pointing a trembling finger behind her. Luna looked back. Behind her on the wall was yet another portrait of her grandfather. He scowled at her, his glare as disapproving as it was in life.

"Granddad?" said Luna. "But it can't be, Sonny ... Granddad's *gone*."

"Not Granddad ... him!" Sonny cried. Luna looked over her other shoulder to see Skeleton Keys appear at the door.

"Who, me?" said the skeleton.

"No, him!" Sonny howled. "Him!"

Luna looked at her shoulder to see her pet rat peering blankly back at her.

"Well, *this* is awkward," said the rat.

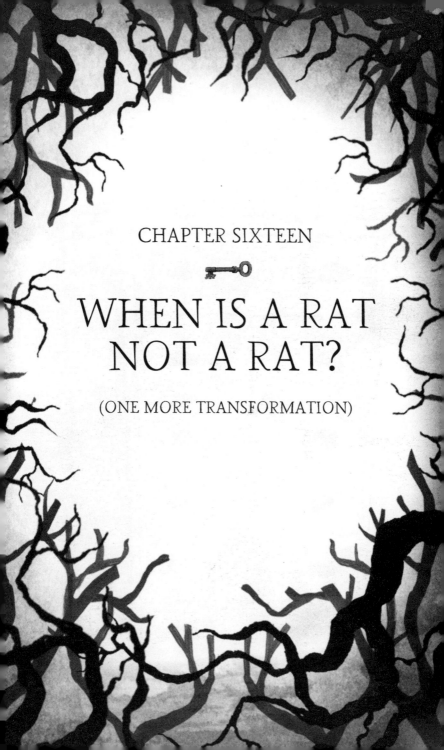

CHAPTER SIXTEEN

WHEN IS A RAT NOT A RAT?

(ONE MORE TRANSFORMATION)

Unimaginaries may be hiding in plain sight!
It is far from simple to know what creatures began their
existence as a figment of the imagination. I recently met a
poodle who promised me she was not unimaginary.
I still have my doubts...

S imon Parker had *spoken*.

Luna's eyes grew wide, and then:

"waa**ah!**"

She screamed and flinched so sharply that
Simon Parker was flung from her shoulder.
The rat landed awkwardly on a nearby chest
of drawers.

"So it turns out I'm a chatty ratty!" said the
rat, standing up on his back legs and dusting
himself off with a tiny front paw. "I was going
to tell you in the end, moonbeam, honest..."

"A talking rodent!" noted Skeleton Keys.

"That is a flabbergasting first – apart from that giant squirrel that told me to—"

"Simon Parker, you can *talk*?" Luna interrupted, aghast.

"Of course I can talk, moonbeam – how else could I be the voice in your ear?" Simon Parker replied.

"Voice? Wait, the voice I kept hearing was you?" Luna said.

"What better place to be a voice in your ear than perched right there on your shoulder?" said Simon Parker, doing a rather smug dance on his back legs. "*Serves her right ... that'll teach him ... he had it coming*," he said, in a rasping growl. "I got the old man's voice down to a tee! I'm also a passable jazz baritone, but I don't like to show off..."

"Crumcrinkles! I do declare that this rat is *unimaginary*," said Skeleton Keys, the revelation hitting him like a brick. "Just as I always suspected."

"Of *course* I'm unimaginary," the rat replied. "Whoever heard of a talking rat?"

"I did once meet a peculiarly poetic porcupine," said Skeleton Keys. He took a bow and added, "It is uncertainly a pleasure to meet you. My name is—"

"Oh, I know who you are!" declared the rat. "I've been watching you since you invited yourself into Haggard Hall ... you and that pesky, back-to-front partner of yours. Although she's a little harder to keep an eye on than you, isn't she...?"

Skeleton Keys glanced to his left to see an empty space where Daisy stood a moment ago. "Cheese 'n' biscuits, *now* where has she gone? That scabbering sidekick is nothing but trouble..." he said. Then he took a moment to compose himself and added, "While we await her up-turning, would you mind telling me exactly who unimagined you? After all, it was Luna's unimaginary family that sent my twitch all itchy-twitchy."

"Oh, I'm not like *them* – I've been here a long time. Longer than anyone, except the boy who imagined me in the first place." Simon Parker pointed a little claw up at the painting on the wall. "The boy who became Old Man Moon."

"*Granddad* unimagined you?" Luna whispered. "But he never even mentioned you! I thought you were just a rat – I *hid* you from him..."

"Don't feel bad, moonbeam. Truth is, I've been hiding from Old Man Moon for a *lifetime*," said Simon Parker. "But turns out, it's almost over! This is the last act, the big finish! Then everything goes back to the way it should be – just you and me."

"He turned Mum into ice! He said he

was going to turn me into a sunflower!"
whimpered Sonny, retreating further under
the bed.

"Is – is that true?" Luna said, putting herself
between Sonny and Simon Parker.

The rat shrugged, and gave a nod. "I did it
for you, moonbeam! So many transformations
… and don't forget that suit of armour I
brought to life. Casting spells and making
magic, that's me! Think I'll need a *spell* of rest
after this…"

"It – it was all you," Luna gasped, the
realization making her weak at the knees. She
steadied herself against her grandfather's bed.
"How? *Why?*"

"Because you don't need them! You've
got the best friend you'll ever have, right
here! Sure, you named me Simon Parker
but that's not how I came into this world.
Hang on to your hat, moonbeam, you won't

believe your eyes..."

The air around Simon Parker began to spark and fizz, and a vortex of silvery smoke appeared from nowhere to circle him. The smoke swirled around the rat, lifting him off his feet and into the air. He hovered above the floor, the smoke whirling faster ... the light show becoming ever more dazzling.

Then, with a final, blinding *FWASH!* of light and silver smoke, Simon Parker the rat was gone ... and floating in his place was a strange, round creature, dressed in a robe peppered with a hundred glinting stars. He was a good deal shorter than Luna and shaped rather like an egg. His skin was milk-white, with eyes like black marbles and a mouth so wide that it resembled a letterbox. On his head was a pointed hat as tall as the fellow himself and covered with as many sparkling stars as his robes.

"Dogs 'n' cats!" cried Skeleton Keys. "An eleventh-hour entrant in our theatre of mystery!"

"Who – who are you?" Luna asked.

"I'm the wiz that is! The magician in position!" the strange, floating man said. "I'm the big deal, the real reveal, the one, the only *Mr Malarkey, the Marvellous Magical Man!*"

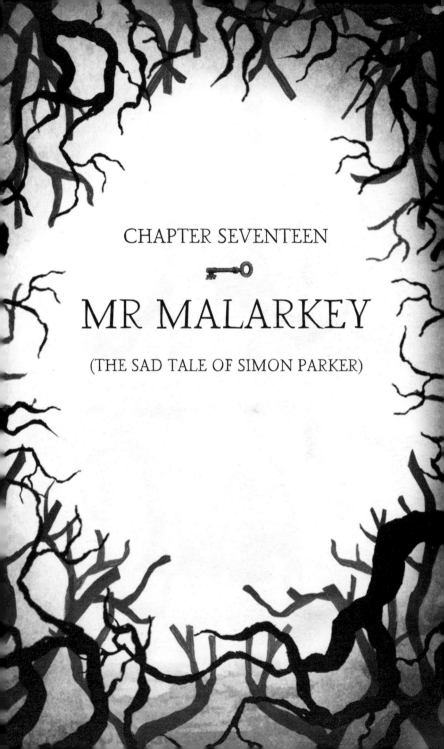

CHAPTER SEVENTEEN

MR MALARKEY

(THE SAD TALE OF SIMON PARKER)

"There is nothing more magical
than a wild imagination!
Except a wizard."
—SK

There was a long, awkward pause as the strange, oval-shaped unimaginary hung, suspended in the air. Finally Skeleton Keys coughed and scratched his head.

"Mr ... Malarkey?" Skeleton Keys repeated, tapping his chin thoughtfully. "I am afraid the name is not ring-dinging any bells..."

"This is the *real* me – the me that Old Man Moon unimagined," explained Mr Malarkey. "That was seventy long years ago. The old man was just a boy back then, all alone in this shadow of a house, but he wasn't alone

for long. In a FLASH! there I was, Mr
Malarkey, the magical maestro!"

"And I never came looking for you?"
Skeleton Keys remarked. "It is possible my
twitch was not always the highly tuned, fool-
proof *unimaginary detector* it is today..."

"As soon as I appeared, I vowed to wow, to
razzle and dazzle the boy with my wondrous
wizardry," continued Mr Malarkey with
arms outstretched. "I gave him whatever he
wanted! I changed this into that, transformed
that into this, turned the other into who-
knows-what ... I even changed myself!
SHAZOO!"

In a flash of light and smoke, Mr Malarkey

was suddenly
replaced with a
rubber beach
ball, hovering
in the air.

"WISK!" he cried, and with another burst of energy, Mr Malarkey became a bicycle. Then, "PLEEM!", he was a rocking horse.

Finally, with a "BLOON!", Mr Malarkey reappeared as the oval-shaped magical man.

"I thought he was happy to have me! And maybe he was ... for a while," Mr Malarkey went on. "But then that black heart of his started to show itself. "*Go on, get out!*" he said. "*This is my house, not yours... Leave me here alone!*" I wasn't

welcome here any more. But it was too late –
I was real! What was I supposed to do? Where
was I supposed to go? I wouldn't even have
existed if it wasn't for him! So I pretended to
disappear. PUFF! But instead I turned
into this..."

Luna squinted at another flash of light.
In an instant Mr Malarkey had once again
become the white rat she'd known as Simon
Parker.

"You have been at Haggard Hall all this
time?" asked Skeleton Keys.

"A *lifetime*," replied the rat, floating
impossibly in the air. "I hid away in the
shadows, waiting ... hoping that the boy
might change his mind. Hoping he might
miss his ol' pal Mr Malarkey and call out for
me, and I'd be there in a flash! But he never
did. He just got older and his soul just got
blacker." The rat floated over to Luna, who

flinched backwards. "But then you came along and found me, moonbeam! What a pair we were – two lonely souls, both stuck with the old man, but both so alone. Well, we weren't so alone when we were together!"

"I didn't know," said Luna, cold with dread. "Why didn't you tell me who you were?"

"I didn't mean to mislead, moonbeam ... I just couldn't risk Old Man Moon finding out I'd never left," the rat replied. "Then, when the old man was gone, I thought I didn't have to hide any more! I thought I could tell you who I *really* was and we could be the friends we were always meant to be – best friends forever!"

"But ... you *tricked* me," said Luna. "You made me think Granddad was haunting me!"

"Oh, that," said the rat, with a shrug. "So, I was a *little* sneaky ... but I knew all this would look better coming from the old man. I mean, he didn't like anyone – who better to banish your fake family forever?"

"My family?" said Luna. "What's this got to do with them?"

"You have to ask?" replied the rat. "I waited *years* for a friend, and you were the friend I'd been waiting for! But then no sooner had the old man gone, than you had to go and unimagine *them*. So I did what I *had* to do – a little FWIM here, a little KA-ZAP there – one minute they're people and the next they're a painting ... a book ... a tin of soup! And I amazed even myself with that spell-tacular suit of armour! I mean, I wasn't even in the same *room* for that trick – do you think that's easy? Well, it is if you're me!"

"I freely admit I did not enjoy that particular rumbleshoving one bit," confessed Skeleton Keys.

"But I don't understand!" Luna blurted.

"Why would you want to do all those horrible things to ... to my family?"

"'Cause it was supposed to be just you and me!" the rat cried. "You and me, best friends forever!"

"That's not how friendship works!" screeched Luna. "You can't just get rid of people because you don't like—"

"Old Man Moon got rid of me!" snapped the rat. "Now I'm going to get rid of them. And we're almost at the encore! Four down, one to go!"

"Wait!" Luna cried as a flash of bright smoke filled the air and Mr Malarkey was restored to his true form. A panicking Sonny scrabbled out from under the bed into Luna's arms. Luna hugged him tightly as Mr Malarkey floated towards them, smoke swirling around him, his hands sparking with energy.

"Bread 'n' butter, that is quite enough of that!" declared Skeleton Keys, sliding between Mr Malarkey and brandishing his keys like weapons. "Yours is a tragic tale, Mr Malarkey, but I nevertheless contend that you have behaved in an unmannerly fashion. I have been dealing with unruly unimaginaries since

before you were a glint in a mind's eye. I have a trick or ten at the tips of my fingers, the likes of which even a marvellous magical man has never seen. So, if you want to get to these children, you will have to go through me first."

"That," said Mr Malarkey with an evil grin, "will be my pleasure."

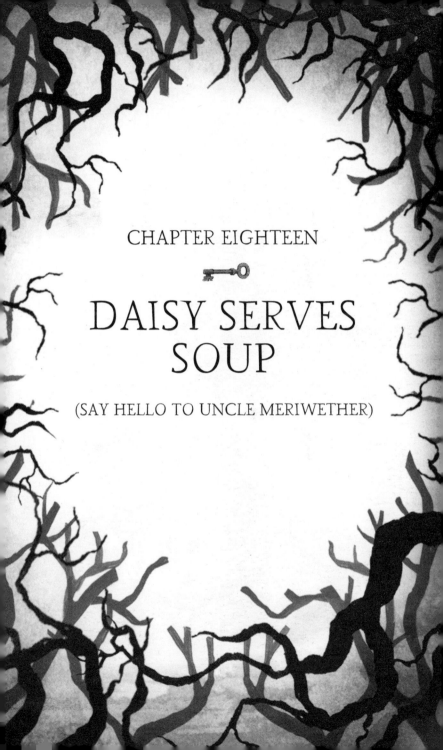

CHAPTER EIGHTEEN

DAISY SERVES SOUP

(SAY HELLO TO UNCLE MERIWETHER)

*"Some unimaginaries have to be seen to be believed.
Especially the invisible ones."*

—SK

"You want to get in my way, skeleton
man?" Mr Malarkey laughed. "I've got
more than enough magic to go round!"

"Do your worst, you rottering rugslug—
AARGH!" Skeleton Keys screamed as a blast
of sparks shot out from Mr Malarkey's hands.
The skeleton ducked and the blast struck Old
Man Moon's bed with a shuddering blow. In a
flash the bed was no more and in its place was
a small toy boat.

"There's more where that came from!" cried
Mr Malarkey, releasing another enchanted

bolt across the room. "I'm the marvellous magical man!"

"I suppose there is a *slim* chance I am hopelessly outmatched," admitted Skeleton Keys, ducking again. "But you forget I have an ace up my bony sleeve – *a trusty assistant*. Now, Daisy! Get him!"

There was a pause.

A long, awkward pause.

"That is it, no more sidekicks!" huffed Skeleton Keys. "I am going it alone! From now on, I am a one-man-bone-band!"

"Uh, may I continue?" asked Mr Malarkey.

"Actually, I would just as soon you did not," replied Skeleton Keys. "I think a quick getaway may be in order..." With that, the skeleton grabbed Luna by one hand and Sonny by the other and made a race for the door, but Mr Malarkey swooped across the room to block their path.

"Leave us alone!" yelled Luna.

"This is the only way, moonbeam! You'll see, we'll be best friends again, just the two of us!" said Mr Malarkey, taking aim at Sonny. "This is where the magic happens! GWAM!"

As a sparkling blast shot out of his hands, Skeleton Keys threw himself in its path. In a bright, blinding instant, he seemed to vanish before Luna's eyes. But even before the smoke had cleared...

"Ba-kawk!"

Luna's mouth fell open. Where once stood Skeleton Keys was the small skeleton of a chicken, dressed in a tiny red tailcoat and looking altogether confused. The skeleton-chicken let out a series of panicked clucks.

"I'd say you just went down in the *pecking* order," laughed Mr Malarkey. He spun round to face Luna and Sonny. "Now, where was I? Oh yeah, the last of the fake family..."

"Please, don't!" Luna cried, holding Sonny tightly. "We – we can all be friends! We can *all* be a family!"

"All of us?" said Mr Malarkey, hovering over them, his black marble eyes glinting in the moonlight.

"Why not?" replied Luna, desperately trying not to sound scared. "There's more than enough room in Haggard Hall. We could *all* stay here."

"We could ... except then I'd have to share," Mr Malarkey said, gritting every last tooth in his letterbox mouth. He took aim at Sonny, his hands glowing with magical energy once more. "It's just going to be you and me from now on, moonbeam. The kid has got to—"

DONK!

"OoWw!"

A tin of soup struck Mr Malarkey in the back of the head, throwing his aim off and sending a magical bolt whizzing past Sonny's head.

"Who threw that?" snapped Mr Malarkey, wheeling round.

"*Serves you right,*" said a disembodied voice. Another tin flew out of nowhere, careening into Mr Malarkey's left ear.

"Oww! Stop that!" moaned the marvellous magical man.

"*That'll teach you,*" the voice said.

"Who said that? Who's there?" Mr Malarkey growled. A third tin sent him spinning around. "Oww! Knock it off!"

"*You had it coming,*" said the voice.

"Stop it!" Mr Malarkey howled. Then he whirled round and stared, wide-eyed at the portrait of Old Man Moon, a flash of fear in his black marble eyes. "It can't be you ... can it?"

"*Course not, egg-head ... but I made you look,*" said the voice as Daisy appeared in the doorway. She produced a tin of soup from behind her front (since her back faced the other direction entirely) and grinned. "Say hello to Uncle Meriwether."

The girl with the backwards head turned

and flung the soup as hard as she could. It flew through the air and landed with an unforgiving *DONK!* right between Mr Malarkey's eyes.

"URFF!" he cried. The magical man spun across the room like a deflating balloon and crashed into a shadowy corner.

"That's for setting a suit of armour on us, egg-head," said Daisy with a lopsided grin.

"Buk!" said Skeleton Keys, flapping his bone wings. "Buk-buk-kawk?"

"What do you mean, where have I been?" replied Daisy. "Unlike you, I don't just rush in without a plan to— Wait, how come I understand what you're saying?"

"Buk-uk, buk-buk?" Skeleton Keys replied.

"Because of our deep mutual respect and understanding?" Daisy scoffed. "Dream on, bird-brain."

"Can we please get out of here?" Luna shrieked, grabbing Sonny and pulling him towards the doorway.

"That's the first not-stupid thing you've said all night," said Daisy, and glanced down at Skeleton Keys. "Come on, you bony bird, let's get out of—"

"You're not going *anywhere*..."

Everyone turned to see Mr Malarkey float up from the floor, sparking and flashing with magical energy. "It was supposed to be me and moonbeam, best friends forever, but you all had to come here and *change* everything," he snarled. "Well, no one does change like me ... you'll see!"

Mr Malarkey began to grow. In a moment he had tripled in size, shredding his star-peppered robes. But he did not *just* grow. As smoke swirled around him the marvellous magical man began to change. His letterbox mouth was suddenly filled with sharp fangs ... from his head sprouted a pair of large, curved horns ... a second pair of arms suddenly emerged from his back ... jagged claws grew from his hands and, finally, thick white hair sprouted all over his body. In a matter of seconds, Mr Malarkey had become a monster.

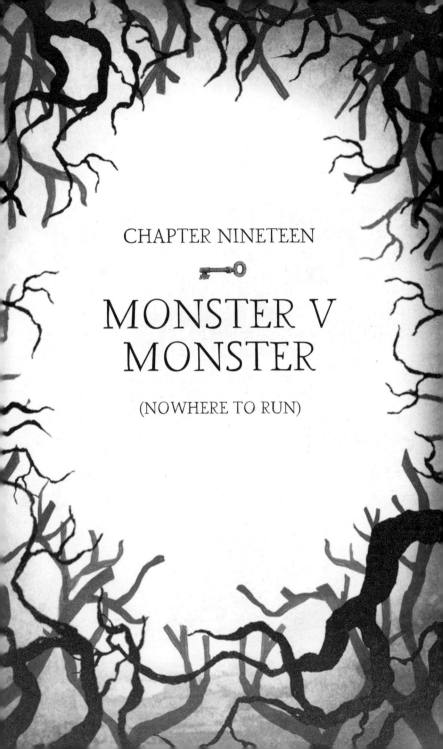

CHAPTER NINETEEN

MONSTER V MONSTER

(NOWHERE TO RUN)

To explain the Key to Reality
For the purposes of clarity
Countless different worlds await!
(With a touch of similarity).

"WHERE DO YOU THINK YOU'RE GOING?" Mr Malarkey

roared, his voice now a wall-shaking roar. As Luna, Sonny, Daisy and the changed-into-a-chicken Skeleton Keys backed off towards the horridor, the monster floated down to the floor.

"Buk-buk-awk!" said Skeleton Keys, flapping his featherless wings and hopping about nervously as the Mr Malarkey monster stomped slowly towards them on his clawed feet.

"No, I haven't got any more tins of soup," tutted Daisy. "And I'd need a tin as big as a *house* to throw at that thing."

"Get away!" cried Luna, backing towards the door as she squeezed Sonny's hand.

"THERE'S NOWHERE TO RUN, MOONBEAM," snarled the Mr Malarkey monster, all four of his clawed hands slashing at the air. "IF YOU WON'T BE MY FRIEND, THEN I WANT TO BE ALL ALONE..."

"Buk-buk-awk!" clucked Skeleton Keys. He flapped his bone wings in panic, and suddenly noticed something about him hadn't changed. Each wing was tipped with five bony keys.

The skeleton's door-opening digits were intact!

"Buk-buk-buK-awk!" he added, with a cluck of relief. "Buk-kawk!"

"What are you on about?" tutted Daisy as they edged backwards. "If I close the door to the horridor, we're *stuck* in here."

"Buk! Buk-buuuk!" Skeleton Keys insisted, hopping up and down and frantically flapping his useless wings.

"*Fine*," Daisy groaned. "But in five seconds I'm going to be invisible and you'll all get eaten..."

Daisy kicked the door shut, trapping them inside Old Man Moon's bedroom.

"What are you doing?" screamed Luna as Mr Malarkey closed in. Daisy shrugged. Then she plucked Skeleton Keys from the floor and held him up against the lock.

"Buk! Buk-kawk!" clucked the skeleton, thrusting one of his key-tipped feather bones into the lock.

"*The Key to Reality?*" repeated Daisy. Then her lopsided grin appeared on her face. "*Oh yeah.*"

As the shadow of the Mr Malarkey monster loomed over them, Skeleton Keys turned the key with a *CLICK CLUNK* and swung open the door.

"BLOOAR!"

"WHAT—?" is all the Mr Malarkey monster had time to say before a giant, green tentacle snaked out of the door and wrapped around his waist. Its suckers fixed to him like glue and squeezed. Mr Malarkey roared and clawed at the tentacle with all four arms, but to no avail. With a defiant "NOOOooooOOOoooo!" from Mr Malarkey, the coiled limb pulled him through the doorway and they disappeared.

"The World Where Absolutely Everything Is a Monster – just where you belong," said

Daisy, kicking the door shut. "Make yourself at home, you witless wizard."

There was a flash and a loud *POP!* as Skeleton Keys was suddenly returned to his usual form. Daisy dropped him to the floor like a stone.

"Bread 'n' butter – Ol' Mr Keys is his handsome self again," the skeleton noted, rubbing his hands over his skull. "What a grinnering relief for everyone!"

"I'm not going to lie," tutted Daisy. "I preferred you as a chicken."

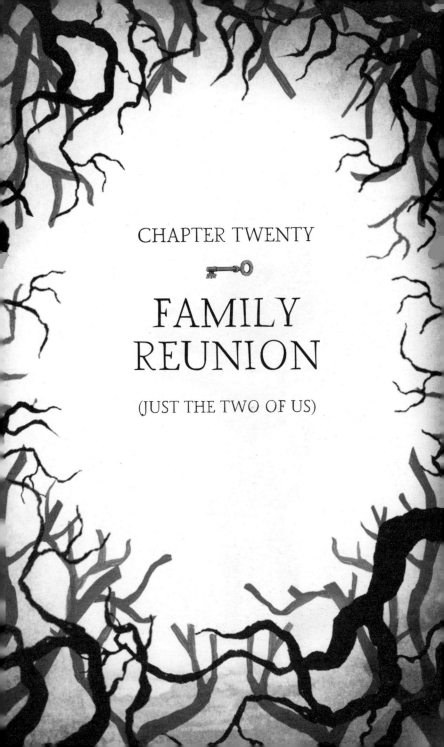

CHAPTER TWENTY

FAMILY
REUNION

(JUST THE TWO OF US)

From *Ol' Mr Keys' Unimaginable Adventures, No. 1,012 –*
The Sort-of Haunting of Luna Moon

A tale of frights 'n' foes 'n' friends!
A monster met a monstrous end!
Luna's secret, now revealed
And bitter feelings quickly healed
Now those that were imaginary
Are Luna's brand-new family!

"Is – is he really gone?" asked Luna, squeezing Sonny so tightly he could barely breathe. Skeleton Keys pulled open the door to the horridor – it was free of Mr Malarkey and monsters and possessed portraits. In fact, an early dawn light trickled in from the landing, making the horridor look altogether less horrifying.

"He is gone," said Skeleton Keys. He looked down at his hands which, but a moment ago, were bony chicken wings. "And it appears his enchantments may have gone with him."

"Looks like it," said Daisy, pointing to a tin of soup on the floor, which had started to rattle and roll. Then with a *POP!* and a flash of light the can was transformed, leaving a confused Uncle Meriwether in its place.

"What was I saying?" Uncle Meriwether said, rubbing his belly. "Something about cake..."

"Uncle Meriwether!" Luna cried, rushing into his arms.

"Well, I'm pleased to see you too, sunbeam!" chuckled Uncle Meriwether as Sonny joined them for a cuddle. "Do you know, I have the oddest taste in my mouth," he added, smacking his lips together. "Tastes like ... *soup.*"

"I'll explain later," said Luna, happy tears welling in her eyes. Her arms shaking with relief, she gave Sonny and Uncle Meriwether the biggest hug she could muster.

"Big hugs to warm us up! Someone let the

cold in..." said a familiar voice. Luna glanced down the horridor to see Mum hurrying towards them, closely followed by Dad and Aunt Summer. They had been returned to human form in the instant Mr Malarkey met his monstrous fate.

"M-Mum? Dad?" Luna cried as happy tears rolled down her face. "Aunt Summer!"

Luna managed to run down the horridor without letting go of Sonny and Uncle Meriwether. They met in the middle in the biggest group hug that Skeleton Keys and Daisy had ever seen.

"Ugh," Daisy said. "I'd rather be sent to the World Where Absolutely Everything Is a Monster than see one more hug."

"That can be arranged," chuckled Skeleton Keys.

"So, you reckon Glumbelina's going to tell her family they're unimaginary?" asked Daisy.

"I expect it will come up, in time ...
and time is something they have," said
Skeleton Keys. For a long moment, the two
unimaginaries watched Luna embrace her
new family, happy tears streaming down
the girl's face, laughter echoing down the
horridor. "Although I cannot imagine they
will hug any less as a result," the skeleton
added.

"In that case, let's get out of here," said
Daisy, without taking her eyes off the family.
Skeleton Keys scratched the back of his skull
and took what may have been a deep breath.

"A grinnering idea," he said. Then he
pushed a key-tipped finger into the lock ...
and paused. "Daisy, perhaps it is all this talk
of family and friendship, but I want you to
know, I am eternally grateful for your help –

231

and your friendship – such as it is."

"Firstly, we're not friends, I'm your *partner*," corrected Daisy. "Second, you're a bone-headed bird-brain who wouldn't last a day without me." A lopsided grin flashed across her face, just for a moment. "So, it's probably best if we stick together for now ... just the two of us."

"I could not agree more," said Skeleton Keys, his toothy grin fixed to his face. With that, he turned his finger with a *CLICK CLUNK*. "Onwards then!" he declared, opening the door. "Onwards, to the next adventure!"

So there we have it, dallywanglers! The truly unbelievable, unbelievably true tale of the sort-of haunting of Luna Moon. Did I not tell you it was a hum-dum-dinger? Families and friends, just like imaginations, do seem to come in all shapes and sizes. And let us never take them for granted, lest they turn us into a tin of soup.

Well, Ol' Mr Keys' work is never done – I already feel the twitch in my bones. Who knows where it will lead? Perhaps to a tale so truly unbelievable that it must, unbelievably, be true. For it has been said, and it cannot be denied, that strange things can happen when imaginations run wild...

Until next time, until next tale, farewell!

Your servant in storytelling,

—SK

WANT TO FIND OUT ABOUT
SKELETON KEYS' NEXT ADVENTURE:

THE LEGEND OF
GAPTOOTH JACK?

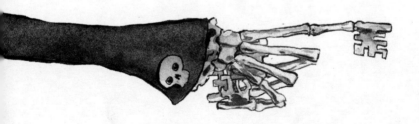

TURN THE PAGE TO FIND OUT...

reetings! To tick-tockers, swiss-cheesers and hurlypots! To the imaginary and the unimaginary! To the living, the dead and everyone in between, my name is Keys ... Skeleton Keys.

Ages or so ago, long before you were even thinking about being born, I was an IF – an imaginary friend. Then, before I knew what was happening, I was suddenly as real as a dog's tail! I had become *unimaginary*.

But that was a lifetime or three ago. Nowadailies, I concern myself with those IFs who have been recently *unimagined*. Wherever they may appear, so does Ol' Mr Keys! For these fantabulant fingers open doors to anywhere and elsewhere ... hidden worlds ... secret places ... doors to the limitless realm of all imagination.

O, glorious burden! These keys have opened

more doors than you have had biscuits – and each door has led to an adventure that would make a head spin from its neck! The stories I could tell you...

But of course you would not be here if you did not want a story! Well, never fear, dallywanglers – today I have a hum-dum-dinger of a tale to make even the soundest mind loop-de-loop! Brace your breeches for the truly unbelievable, unbelievably true tale I have called *The Legend of Gaptooth Jack*.

Ah, Gaptooth Jack – Thief! Adventurer! Champion of imagining! Jack was a friend to some, hero to others, and a right pain in the rumplings for everyfolk else. The flabbergasting fable of Gaptooth Jack is even older than I, but to find our way to the past we must begin in the present, with a *second* story, and a boy named Kasper.

Kasper has what we in the business of

imagining call a *wild imagination*. On the
seventh day of his seventh year, Kasper
imagined himself a friend. He did not *need*
to, perhaps, for he had friends enough. But
imaginations are not trussed 'n' tethered by
need ... imaginations run free! Kasper named
his IF *Wordy Gerdy*. Gerdy was a ghost of
a girl with a most remarkable ability – with
pen in hand she could rewrite the story of
life itself. Let us suppose you have a pet
dog – if Wordy Gerdy rewrote your story,
you might suddenly have a cat instead. And,
what is more, you would not even know
that anything had changed – you would be
as sure as shampoo that you had *always* had
a cat!

Now imagine if Wordy Gerdy became
unimaginary ... if her power to rewrite stories
became real. What then is to stop chaos,
confusion or even calamity? For strange

things can happen when imaginations run wild...

Join me as I begin to unravel the mystery of the myth of the legend of Gaptooth Jack, by first paying a much-needed visit to Kasper and his family. Their tiny house, dwarfed by the sprawling city that surrounds it, shuddles 'n' shakes as a thunderstorm rages outside. The story has just begun, and yet it has already been re-written...

Guy Bass is an award-winning author and
semi-professional geek. He has written over thirty books,
including the best-selling *Stitch Head* series (which has been
translated into sixteen languages) *Dinkin Dings and the
Frightening Things* (winner of a 2010 Blue Peter Book Award)
*Spynosaur, Laura Norder: Sheriff of Butts Canyon, Noah Scape
Can't Stop Repeating Himself, Atomic!* and *The Legend of Frog*.

Guy has previously written plays for both adults and children.
He lives in London with his wife and imaginary dog.
Find out more at guybass.com

Pete Williamson is a self-taught artist and illustrator.
He is best known for the much-loved *Stitch Head* series by
Guy Bass, and the award-winning *The Raven Mysteries*
by Marcus Sedgwick.

Pete has illustrated over sixty-five books by authors including
Francesca Simon, Matt Haig and Charles Dickens. Before that
he worked as a designer in an animation company (while
daydreaming about being a children's book illustrator).

Pete now lives in rural Kent with a big piano, a writer wife and
a dancing daughter. Find out more at petewilliamson.co.uk

Have you read *Stitch Head*?

'It's dark, monstrous fun!' Wondrous Reads

In Castle Grotteskew something BIG
is about to happen to someone SMALL.
Join a mad professor's first creation as
he steps out of the shadows into the
adventure of an almost lifetime...

Read all Stitch Head's adventures:

The Pirate's Eye

The Ghost of Grotteskew

THE SPIDER'S LAIR

The Beast of Grubbers Nubbin

THE MONSTER HUNTER

BRINGING THE CHARACTERS TO LIFE

Guy and Pete explain how the characters evolved...

Luna Moon

GB: Pete did a few sketches of Luna and one immediately stood out – she looked spot on.

PW: As soon as I drew her she stood out for me too, and I was really hoping Guy would choose her.

GB: The way I described her meant she looked a bit too much like Ben Bunsen from the first Skeleton Keys book, so we changed her hair from black to white.

I love the way she turned out.

Simon Parker

PW: A friend had been putting pictures of her pet white rat up on social media so they came in very useful when drawing Simon.

GB: We looked at a few different colour options (I had no idea rats came in so many colours) but when we changed Luna's hair, a white Simon Parker seemed like a neat match.

Pete did some fantastic sketches of Luna's rat sniffing around Haggard Hall. The more realistic he looked, the more I liked him.

Mr Malarkey

GB: I imagined the Marvellous Magical Man as a sort of floating Humpty Dumpty in a wizard's outfit. Pete's initial design made him a bit more human and appealing but the final design was stranger, which I loved. I especially like his monstrous form. I have a thing for characters turning into monsters.

PW: When I draw monsters I always forget I'm drawing for children and I just try and come up with something that would horrify me (and hopefully Guy) and this is what came out. Lots of razor sharp black claws, rows of terrible teeth and a very bad mood.

SKELETON KEYS WILL RETURN